THE DRAGON
AT THE
NORTH POLE

DRAGON KEEPERS

DRAGON KEEPERS 🐉 BOOK 6

THE DRAGON
AT THE
NORTH POLE

KATE KLIMO

with illustrations
by
JOHN SHROADES

Random House 🏠 New York

For Jim Thomas,
honorary Dragon Keeper

Text copyright © 2013 by Kate Klimo
Jacket art and interior illustrations copyright © 2013 by John Shroades

Visit us on the Web!
randomhouse.com/kids

Educators and librarians, for a variety of teaching tools, visit us at
RHTeachersLibrarians.com

For more Dragon Keepers fun, go to TheDragonKeepers.com and FoundaDragon.org

Library of Congress Cataloging-in-Publication Data
Klimo, Kate.
The dragon at the North Pole / Kate Klimo ;
with illustrations by John Shroades. — First edition.
pages cm. — (Dragon keepers ; book 6)
Summary: Using magic snowshoes, cousins Jesse and Daisy travel to the North Pole
to retrieve their pet dragon.
ISBN 978-0-375-87066-8 (trade) — ISBN 978-0-375-97066-5 (lib. bdg.) —
ISBN 978-0-307-97438-9 (ebook) — ISBN 978-0-375-87117-7 (pbk.)
[1. Dragons—Fiction. 2. Magic—Fiction. 3. Santa Claus—Fiction. 4. Christmas—Fiction.
5. Cousins—Fiction.] I. Shroades, John, illustrator. II. Title.
PZ7.K67896 Dn 2013 [Fic]—dc23 2012041171

Printed in the United States of America
10 9 8 7 6 5 4 3 2 1
First Edition

CONTENTS

THE WORLD
IS TALKING TO US.
EVERYTHING IN IT
HAS A STORY TO TELL.
ALL WE HAVE TO DO
IS SIT QUIETLY
AND LISTEN.
THIS STORY BEGINS
WITH A SNOWFALL.

Chapter One

ALODIE'S ALLEY

Dear Mom and Dad, I hope my package arrived safely. Don't open it until tomorrow morning. (Although it's practically tomorrow there now anyway!) It's your Christmas present from me and Daisy. I won't spoil the

surprise, but I will say that Daisy and I made
it. The only hint I'll give is that we whipped it
up in the blender! Uncle Joe and Aunt Maggie
are having a big Christmas Eve party today,
just for grown-ups, but that's okay because
Daisy and I had already planned to go to the
grand opening of a new shop in town. It is
called Alodie's Alley. The store belongs to our
friend who lives down the street, the lady
with the awesome garden I told you about.
I have to go now because Daisy is yelling for
me. The party is *super* loud. Must be Uncle
Joe's Killer-Diller Loosey-Goosey Eggnog.

Daisy yelled again. Jesse hollered back through
the open door of his bedroom, "Down in a minute!"
Wishing his parents—who were in Africa—a merry
Christmas, he clicked SEND, switched off the old
desktop computer, and waited while the screen
blinked and twitched and finally sputtered out.
Then he slipped his backpack on over his hoodie
and made his way downstairs.

Jesse had spent most of his life living outside of
America, in places where Doctors Without Borders
posted his parents. Last spring, a little after his
tenth birthday, he had come to live with his ten-
year-old cousin, Daisy, in America, in the little

northwestern town of Goldmine City. Not long after that, he and his cousin had become the Keepers of a very fast-growing baby dragon named Emerald—Emmy, for short.

Jesse wished Emmy could see the house. Aunt Maggie had really gone all out decorating the place, winding Christmas lights around the stair railing and even decking the halls with fresh boughs of holly. Emmy would love it. This being Emmy's first Christmas, she was as keyed up as a kid in a candy store. Emmy lived in the barn behind the house, the only space big enough for a seven-month-old dragon who had, for the time being (and much to their relief), leveled off to the size of two full-grown elephants. The rule was she was not supposed to reveal herself to anyone but her Keepers, not even at Christmastime.

Carols blasted on the sound system in the living room. The guests, holding foaming cups of eggnog, laughed and talked and spilled out into the down-stairs hallway. Jesse worked his way through the crowd toward the corner of the living room where the Christmas tree sparkled.

Jesse found Aunt Maggie near the fireplace, wearing one of her prettiest dresses. She was of-fering a platter of sesame crackers smeared with goat cheese to a rather skinny-looking Santa Claus and a woman Jesse didn't recognize at first because he had never seen her out of uniform: Ms. Mindy, the dogcatcher.

"Merry Christmas, everybody," Jesse said.

When Jesse started to help himself to the crackers with both hands, Aunt Maggie gave him a narrow look and said, "Isn't Miss Alodie offering refreshments at her grand opening?"

Jesse nodded as he swallowed a mouthful of pure deliciousness. "Why do you think I'm eating now?" Miss Alodie had some very strange ideas about food.

Aunt Maggie laughed.

The man dressed as Santa Claus said in a deep voice, "Ho-ho-ho, save some for Santa Claus! Remember, I still have my rounds to make later tonight." Hiding beneath the fake white beard was Mr. Stinson, the weekday librarian at the Goldmine City Public Library.

"I meant to ask," Jesse said with a grin. "How do your reindeer pull the sled if there isn't any snow on the ground?"

Ms. Mindy said, "Oh, Santa finds ways. He has to because it never snows in Goldmine City."

"At least not more than a dusting," added Aunt Maggie.

Ms. Mindy said, "This year it's so warm you can

go without a coat. I feel sorry for the dogs stifling in their winter fur."

"Well, you never know," Aunt Maggie said with a wink at Jesse. "Maybe we're in for a Christmas miracle."

There were times when Aunt Maggie reminded Jesse so much of his mother that it made him just the tiniest bit homesick. "Maybe," Jesse said with a shy shrug.

"Don't you worry, young man," Mr. Stinson said to Jesse, his eyes twinkling. "Whatever the weather, Santa always comes through."

Jesse did his best to twinkle back. It had been years since he had believed in Santa. Number one, outside of America, Santa wasn't such a big deal. Number two, his parents were scientists and didn't encourage such beliefs. And number three, Santa was for *little* kids. And he wasn't a little kid. He was a Dragon Keeper. Still, he hadn't believed in dragons before Emmy hatched out of her geode, so who knew?

"I think I hear Daisy calling," Jesse said as he popped one more sesame cracker in his mouth, pocketed another, and wended his way back through the throng.

"*There* you are!" said Daisy, jumping up and down with excitement the moment Jesse swung open the kitchen door. She had tied a sparkly blue Christmas garland around her head. The pointy pink tips of her ears poked through her pale blond hair. She wore a red sweater, green jeans, and fuzzy white boots.

"Hey, Jess!" Uncle Joe called out. "You're just in time to crack open the next goose egg." Uncle Joe was working at the kitchen table, where he had set up the blender. His idea of dressing up for Christmas was to tie a red ribbon around his gray ponytail and wear a green T-shirt with red letters that said JINGLE BELL ROCK. Below the letters was a picture of a rock with a Santa hat on it. Uncle Joe was a geologist.

Jesse went over and picked up one of the big gray goose eggs sitting on the table. He cracked it with a butter knife and dumped the gloopy contents into the blender. Daisy poured heavy cream in after it. It felt a little weird to be making something edible in the blender when he and Daisy had spent the last four weeks using it to make paper. After much experimentation, they had used just about everything *but* goose eggs in their paper recipes.

On the table were two festively wrapped cardboard mailing tubes. The one in blue gift wrap contained the paper they had made for Miss Alodie. The red one was Emmy's.

"Poppy, we need to head out to Alodie's Alley now," Daisy said.

"Be back by six-thirty," Uncle Joe said.

Daisy signaled for Jesse to turn around. She fit the two gift-wrapped tubes into his backpack. She couldn't zip it up because the tubes stuck out the top.

Uncle Joe turned on the blender.

Jesse spoke to Daisy under the whirring noise. "Are we giving Emmy her gift now or waiting until after we come back from town?"

"After," Daisy said. "That way we can tuck her in."

"Plan," Jesse said. "She's been bouncing off the walls lately."

Though Emmy was only seven months old, she behaved like a rebellious preteen with a tendency to revert to adorably childlike behavior. For instance, she read movie magazines, but she liked to be tucked in at night. This was fine with Jesse and Daisy. Like most parents, they didn't want their darling to grow up too fast. And tucking her in at night gave them a chance to check up on her.

Uncle Joe switched off the blender. "Hey, what

are you two elves conspiring about?" he asked.

"Nothing!" said Jesse guiltily.

"Wouldn't you like to know?" Daisy said with an innocent look.

As they walked the three blocks to town, Christmas lights began to wink on up and down Nugget Lane. Jesse checked his watch. It was only four o'clock and already nearly dark. They stopped now and then to comment on the lights. Jesse preferred the displays with a few well-placed lights, while Daisy went for the ones that pulled out all the stops. Goldmine City—which had been a mining town at the turn of the nineteenth century—was festooned with garlands of lights crisscrossing Main Street.

When they reached Alodie's Alley, Daisy swung open the door and peered inside. It smelled spicy and exotic.

"Welcome, young friends!" Miss Alodie chirped.

Not much taller than a garden gnome, Miss Alodie was perched on a high stool at the back of the store. She was wearing a purple smock with silver stars on it and, on her wispy white hair, a beanie that looked like the top of an eggplant with the stem still on it. On the counter before her, in place of a cash register, was an abacus with amber beads. Next to that were a pot of herbal tea and a tray of crackers with blue stuff smeared on them. There were crystals hanging from the ceiling, along with bunches of dried herbs and wildflowers tied with colorful ribbons.

There were also wind chimes and dream catchers—*real* ones, not the hokey kind you find in tourist-trap souvenir shops. Tables were draped with colorful shawls displaying stones and gems, blue glass vials containing essential oils, scented beeswax candles and soaps, good-luck charms and talismans, boxes of herbal teas, and jars of jams and bath salts.

"I don't know where to look first!" Daisy said, standing in the middle of the floor.

"I do!" said Jesse, making a beeline for the table holding the stones and gems.

"I knew my alley would be right up your alley!" Miss Alodie said with a chuckle.

Daisy drifted around, sniffing candles, testing wind chimes, and examining the labels of things. When she came upon the small rickety bookcase, she knelt and skimmed the spines, stopping at a thick volume entitled *The Encyclopedia Fantastica: Hobgoblins, Brownies, Trolls, and Other Supernatural Creatures.* She pulled it out, settled down on the floor, and cracked it open.

Most of the books she found that purported to

be about fantastical creatures weren't accurate. The dryads, or tree spirits, looked like space aliens, and the hobgoblins looked like Snow White's dwarves. But in this book, the dryads were pictured as looking like the lumbering, long-haired giants she and Jesse had encountered last spring. And the hobgoblins, which they had met on the same adventure, looked much as she remembered them: anvil-headed little creatures with smashed snouts and three fingers on each hand.

She was going to call Jesse over to show him, when her cousin dashed up to the counter and said, "Can I get this for Emmy? How much does it cost?"

Miss Alodie was the only grown-up in Gold-mine City who knew about their dragon. Daisy sometimes wondered whether Miss Alodie might herself be some sort of magical creature. Certainly, the gifts she gave them were almost always magical.

"Oh, I'm quite sure you can't afford it, young sir," Miss Alodie said to Jesse, taking from his hand a green rock the size of a kiwi fruit. "This happens to be an uncut emerald from the jungles of Sri Lanka. And even if you had the money, I wouldn't take it. Let's just call it a gift from the two of us for Emerald."

Jesse looked stunned. "Really?" he said.

"Truly," said Miss Alodie.

"Fantastica!" Daisy said. When she glanced back down at the book, she saw that it had fallen open to a page about trolls. They had big lumpy heads with sharp fangs and goggle eyes, and long arms and legs with sharp claws. Below the illustration were three words: "Fears live flame."

"Ugly customers. Hope I never run into one of *them*," she muttered to herself. Returning the book to the shelf, she joined Jesse at the counter, where Miss Alodie was telling Jesse about the legendary powers of emeralds.

"Their most valuable property," Miss Alodie was saying, "is that they lose their color in the presence of treachery."

For some reason, this comment made the hair on the back of Daisy's neck stand up.

"Neat," said Jesse. "Emmy will like that, won't she, Daisy?"

Daisy nodded and rubbed her neck.

"And speaking of Emmy," Jesse said, "we'd better get going."

"Right," said Daisy. Then she gasped. "We almost forgot! We haven't given you your present, Miss Alodie!"

Jesse turned around so Daisy could pull the blue tube out of the backpack.

Miss Alodie carefully removed the wrapping

paper and stared, mystified, at the cardboard mailing tube.

"Take out that plastic plug on the end and look inside," Jesse urged her.

Miss Alodie did so and peered inside. "Oh, my!" she said. "What have we here?"

"It's handmade paper!" Daisy said, too excited to wait a second more.

Miss Alodie reached a finger into the tube and carefully pulled out the paper that was rolled up inside. Jesse cleared a spot on the counter so Miss Alodie could flatten the paper. The cousins crowded around.

The texture was rough and the edges were irregular. After mixing up the pulp in the blender, Jesse and Daisy had poured it into a mold they had made from an old screen stretched across a picture frame. The screen drained the moisture and the frame shaped the sheet.

"We did different recipes for different people," Jesse said.

"We put dried flowers in yours. See?" said Daisy, pointing to the fragments of pink rose petals. "You can write on it. Or draw on it."

"Can I *frame* it?" Miss Alodie asked. "A true work of craftsmanship merits a frame."

Jesse and Daisy looked at each other and

shrugged happily. "Sure, why not?" said Jesse.

"Did you know that the Chinese made the first paper?" Miss Alodie asked. "They originally put their inscriptions on bamboo, but bamboo was too heavy and cumbersome. Silk was light but too expensive. So they mashed up rags and wood fiber and pressed a sheet from it. The ancient Egyptians made their paper from mashed papyrus plant, hence the name paper.

"The invention of paper is one of the most profound in the history of the world. Paper makes it possible to communicate, to exchange ideas and currencies, to write books and paint pictures, and to print out the contracts of agreement that bind us to one another. It's a miraculous substance, and you children have brilliantly mastered the making of it. Bravo!" she said. Then she picked up the tray of crackers and thrust it toward them.

Jesse pulled back. The crackers looked like chips of white plaster. They were smeared with a paste as bright blue as pool paint. Nothing about the offering looked like food.

"Help yourselves!" Miss Alodie said.

Jesse smiled gamely and took one, remembering how Miss Alodie's fairy cakes had tasted like dog shampoo. "I'll save it for later," he said, stuffing it into the pouch of his hoodie, where he hoped it wouldn't contaminate Aunt Maggie's sesame cracker with goat cheese.

It was completely dark when Jesse and Daisy stepped outside, which made the street's Christmas lights sparkle all the more brightly. When they arrived back home, the party was still going on but was quieter. They walked down the driveway, cut through the backyard, and crawled through the tunnel in the laurel bushes. When they poked their heads out the other side, they were both so startled by what they saw that they fell backward on their heels.

Chapter Two

SANTA'S HELPER

As if someone had thrown a gigantic switch, the northern horizon shimmered in a dazzling display of green and red light.

Jesse and Daisy exchanged a wordless look. Before they passed through the laurels, they hadn't seen these lights. How had they both missed them?

Emmy was straddling the ridge of the barn's roof. The barn was big, but their dragon covered half of it. Her long, noble snout was tipped toward the heavens.

"Yo, Emmy!" Jesse called up to the dragon.

Emmy looked down at them, her eyes huge and luminous. "Hey! You guys are just in time for the show. . . . I got us front row seats!"

Emmy popped her wings—green on top, purple underneath—and glided down to the tawny grass. She caught them up in her arms and flew them back up to the roof, where she held them, one in the crook of each arm. Jesse took a moment to adjust to the height and then settled in. Like a curtain rippling and billowing in a breeze, the lights shifted and danced.

"Listen!" Emmy said. "Can you hear it?"

Daisy, eyes on the lights, shook her head.

"It's light, not sound waves," said Jesse. "You can't *hear* light. You can only *see* it."

"Oh, this light makes a sound, all right," Emmy said with a canny nod.

All Jesse heard was the wind stirring the trees in the Deep Woods below. "What does it sound like?" he asked.

"Heavenly," Emmy said dreamily. "But I can't make out the words. It's so frustrating!"

Daisy said, "We can't hear anything, Em. We wish we could."

Emmy sighed. "I've been thinking that it's Santa Claus trying to get a message through to me. Maybe he's saying he'll be here as soon as the snow falls."

"Oh, Em," said Jesse. Emmy was so eager. He hated to see her hopes dashed. "Didn't we explain to you that it doesn't snow much here?"

Emmy shook her head. "Nuh-uh. It's going to snow. I can smell it." She lifted her snout to the sky and sniffed. "Come on. Can't you guys smell it?"

Jesse sniffed. "Not really, Em."

"Well, *I* can smell it. It's going to snow. And when it snows, everybody knows"—Emmy burst into song—"Santa Claus is coming to town!"

Jesse said, "Em, we told you that Santa Claus is just a myth for little kids. And you're not a little kid anymore."

"You're a big girl," Daisy added, gesturing at Emmy's double-elephantine bulk. "Very big."

"You guys! You're enough to make me flame sometimes!" Emmy shouted indignantly.

"We're sorry," Jesse said.

"Not sorry enough," Emmy said sulkily. When

she pouted, a single fang poked out on the side of her mouth. Then she shook off the sulk and burst into song again: "I better watch out. I better not cry. I better not pout, I'm telling you why."

"Santa Claus is coming to town," the cousins joined in.

"That's the spirit," said Emmy, looking down at them fondly. "Tell me this: how do you know Santa *isn't* real?"

Jesse shrugged. "We just know, is all."

"What about those lights?" Emmy said. "Green and red are Santa's colors."

Jesse said, "Scientifically speaking, the color is the result of the collision of electrically charged particles with atoms in the high atmosphere. The light that results is known as the aurora borealis, or northern lights in the Northern Hemisphere, and aurora australis in the Southern. But I have to say, it's pretty weird that we can see the northern lights this far south. Usually you can only see them in places like Alaska, Siberia, and Norway."

Jesse had done a report on the northern lights for his science class last year—not that there was actually a "class" when you are an only child being homeschooled in a hut in Africa not much bigger than a toolshed. But he had gotten an A on it.

Emmy didn't seem to be listening. Her head

cocked, she had ears only for the song of the lights.

Jesse tapped her on the shoulder. "Hey, Em, what do you say we get down off this roof so you can unwrap your Christmas presents?"

Emmy snapped to attention. "Why didn't you say so?"

Emmy moved so quickly, Jesse's stomach was still up on the roof when Emmy landed on the grass and set him and Daisy on their feet. She pushed open the barn's sliding door.

"Now this is what I call Christmas magic!" Jesse said, looking around.

An old glass lantern shed a cozy glow on the Museum of Magic, which consisted of old barn planks lying across a couple of sawhorses. It displayed the cousins' ever-growing collection of rocks, skulls, feathers, and mysterious found objects, all of which they believed possessed magical powers. Emmy had cleared a spot on the planks and set up a small fir tree decorated with items from the museum, including bird nests, pinecones, and the Sorcerer's Sphere.

Emmy hunkered down next to the museum and unwrapped her first gift, the cardboard mailing tube wrapped in red. Inside were three sheets of paper made from white rags and dried grass.

Emmy eased the paper out of the tube with a

long green talon. She had told them that dragons came from a place called the Time Before. So the paper Jesse and Daisy had made for her had a sturdy, ancient look that seemed just right.

Daisy pointed to the upper right-hand corner, where in fancy green script she had written "From the Desk of Emerald of Leandra." Beneath it there was a smiley face with two fangs, which had been the way Emmy signed her name when she was little.

"We made you three big sheets," Jesse said. As befitted a nearly full-grown dragon, each sheet was poster-sized.

"Why, thank you!" said Emmy.

"I'll get you my bottle of green ink and maybe you can use a big feather for a quill," Daisy suggested.

"I won't need ink," Emmy said. "I have dragon ichor and talons." Dragon ichor was the green stuff Emmy secreted from her talons.

"And here's a little something from Miss Alodie's new store," said Jesse. He handed her a square box Miss Alodie had wrapped in purple tissue and tied with a green bow.

Emmy took the box and held it in the palm of her hand. "Pretty!" she said, viewing it from all angles.

Daisy cleared her throat. "Em? There's actually something *inside*."

"Oh!" Emmy unwrapped the box and picked out the green stone. In her large palm, it looked no bigger than a pea.

"Just what I always wanted!" she exclaimed. Then she said blankly, "What is it?"

"It's a raw emerald," Jesse said, and went on to tell her about the stone's ability to reveal treachery.

Emmy wasn't listening. Her snout hung low and her tail swept the dusty planks of the barn floor.

"What's wrong?" Daisy asked softly.

"I don't have any gifts to give you," Emmy said sorrowfully. "I was hoping Santa would come to town and give me a hand. But if you say it never snows here . . . Maybe that's what the song coming from the northern lights is saying, that Santa Claus *isn't* coming to town." She looked up, her big green eyes brimming with tears.

"Don't be sad, Emmy," said Daisy. "We don't need presents from you."

"Daisy's right," said Jesse. "Just having you in our lives is the best present we could have."

Slowly, Emmy began to brighten. "Really?"

"Really," said Jesse and Daisy.

Emmy held out her arms to them. "Holiday hug?"

After the hug, Jesse clapped his hands and said, "Okay, Emmy! Time to brush your fangs."

Emmy scowled. "Oh, pooh!" she said.

The cousins followed her outside to the water trough, where she kept the push broom she used for a toothbrush. As she ran the bristles over her fangs, she said, "Why I hafoo oo is?"

"So you won't lose any more fangs," Daisy said. Just after Thanksgiving, Emmy had gotten a terrible fang ache and had lost the fang not long afterward.

Emmy lowered the brush and growled. "Yeah, well, the Fang Fairy ripped me off."

"We've told you, there's no such thing as the Fang Fairy," Jesse said patiently. "Any more than there is such a thing as Santa Claus."

"Then how come she took my fang and didn't leave me a quarter?" Emmy said. She dipped her nose into the trough, slurped up water, tossed back her head, and gargled loudly before spitting the water out.

Jesse and Daisy didn't have a good answer for Emmy. When Emmy had lost her fang, she hadn't told them about it. Instead, she had put the fang under her pillow of socks for the Fang Fairy to find. The next day the fang was missing! But nothing had been left in return.

"The next time you lose a fang, you need to tell

us," Daisy said. "That way we can play at being the Fang Fairy and leave you a quarter."

"I want the *real* Fang Fairy," Emmy said sulkily, "not a play one."

Just like she wanted the real Santa Claus. Jesse sighed. Sometimes being a Dragon Keeper was just impossible.

They walked back to the barn and tucked Emmy into the old corncrib, which was filled with rolled-up socks. She wouldn't let them leave until Jesse had read *A Visit from St. Nicholas*. Then Jesse and Daisy headed back to the house. After a light supper, they went upstairs carrying steaming cups of hot chocolate. A bathroom separated their bedrooms.

"If you wake up first," Daisy said, "come next door to wake me. We're allowed to open our stockings before we eat breakfast."

"Excellent!" said Jesse.

Christmas morning, Jesse woke up to Daisy's finger drilling a hole in his shoulder.

"What?" he muttered groggily. He felt a sudden cold draft on the side of his face.

"Look, Jess!" Daisy said, pointing out the window next to his bed.

Jesse turned and gaped in astonishment.

It was as if someone had come along during the night and smothered the world in whipped cream. Freshly fallen snow covered the ground and the rooftops, weighing down the bushes and tree branches. More snow fell from the sky, which was a soft, pale gray, unlike any sky Jesse had ever seen before.

He sat up and let out a loud whoop of delight.

"Just a dusting, eh?" he said with a chuckle. He pressed his nose to the frigid windowpane. Then he turned to Daisy and said, "Let's go outside!"

Daisy flapped her hands. "I can't wait to see how Emmy likes her first snow!"

They met in the hallway, dressed in long underwear and jeans and sweatshirts and socks. Daisy put her finger to her lips as she led Jesse tiptoeing past the master bedroom. They crept down the stairs and peered into the living room. The tree was brightly lit, and their stockings were stuffed with gifts. More presents were piled beneath the tree.

As much as Jesse would have liked to sit down and unpack his stocking, the snow was calling to him. From the look on Daisy's face, the snow was calling to her, too.

Ten minutes later, in boots and scarves and mittens and winter coats, Jesse and Daisy stepped outside.

"Race you to the Dell!" Daisy said. She leapt off the porch and immediately fell face-first into the snow. She sat up, spitting out snow and laughing. There was no going very fast in this stuff. Jesse dived in after her. He wanted to wallow in it, to pack it into balls, to lie down in it and make snow angels, to touch his tongue to it, to do all the wonderful things he'd never had a chance to do in the tropical places he'd lived. And if *he* was this excited, what would Emmy be doing?

Jesse and Daisy picked up their feet and giant-stepped through the thigh-high drifts. They had to stop every few steps to rest. When they got to the laurel bushes, they slid through the tunnel on their bottoms and struggled to their feet on the other side.

The Dell lay before them, a vast white china bowl with a fine black crack in it where the brook cut through the snow. To the west, Old Mother Mountain rose up like a huge white ghost, mini avalanches tumbling down her steep shoulders. Every branch of every tree in the Deep Woods was coated with snow.

In contrast to all the whiteness, the old dairy barn stood out as if a fresh coat of red paint had been applied to it overnight. The snow banked up against the sides of the barn, pure and undisturbed.

Strangely, Emmy hadn't set foot in it yet.

Jesse and Daisy went slipping and sliding down the hill. When they came to the front of the barn, they stopped short.

"Maybe she was up late," said Daisy.

"Maybe she doesn't even know it snowed," Jesse said.

"Wait till she sees!" said Daisy

But the moment they slid the barn door open, they knew something was wrong. The warmth of Emmy's body normally kept the barn toasty, but this morning the barn was cold. They ran to the corn-crib. It was empty. They climbed up to the loft. Also empty.

Their dragon, Emerald of Leandra, was gone.

When they got back down the ladder, they saw one of the sheets of paper they'd given Emmy the night before spread out on the planks of the Museum of Magic. It was anchored in place by the raw emerald. On her brand-new personal stationery, Emmy had written in her large loopy hand: "Dear J and D, Gone to help Santa. E of L." She had added her two-fanged smiley face.

"'Gone to help Santa'?" Daisy said. "What could that possibly mean?"

"I don't know," Jesse said, bewildered. "But wherever she went, she didn't take her emerald with her." He slipped the gemstone into his coat pocket.

Daisy looked around the barn, her brow furrowed. "What about the other two pieces of stationery?" she asked. "Where are they?"

Jesse shrugged. "Maybe the professor has some ideas. Come on."

They headed back. The trip home wasn't anywhere near as much fun as the trip out. Now the snow was just a cold white obstacle to their urgent need to contact the professor, their adviser on dragon matters.

When they got into the mudroom, they peeled off their layers, then made their way up to Jesse's room. Jesse threw himself into his desk chair and switched on his computer. He sat back and stared at the still-black screen. Behind him, Daisy stood drumming her fingers on the back of his chair.

For Christmas, Jesse had asked his parents for a new computer to replace his old, slow one, but instead they had given him a handheld gizmo called a Blueberry. Jesse called it Blueberry Sal, after a character in one of his favorite picture books, but he still hadn't mastered using the tiny keyboard.

The Blueberry was downstairs in Jesse's backpack. Just as he was beginning to think that he ought to run and get it, the computer came to life with a reluctant *blurp*. After Jesse had typed in www.foundadragon.org, the professor's familiar white-bearded face materialized on the screen. There was a sprig of holly stuck in the lapel of his black coat, and he was holding a cup.

"Happy winter solstice!" Professor Lukas B. Andersson said, raising his cup to toast them.

"You're a little late," Jesse said. "Winter solstice was the twenty-first."

"Actually, it was the twenty-second this year," the professor said. "But why quibble? It is not possible to detect the actual instant of the solstice. In order to pinpoint the day, we must be able to observe a change in azimuth, or elevation, of less than or equal to about one hundred sixty degrees of the angular diameter of the sun."

"What are you two talking about?" Daisy said.

"The winter solstice," Jesse said. "It's the shortest day of the year, when the earth's axis is tipped farthest away from the sun. That's why the sun is so low in the sky and why it's dark in the morning and the late afternoon."

"Yeah, well," said Daisy. "Whatever you want to call it, Emmy took off."

The professor's snowy white brows lowered over his eyes. "Took off *what*?" he asked. "Don't tell me she's taken to wearing habiliments."

"Habiliments?" Daisy said.

"Clothes, I think," said Jesse. Then he said to the professor, "What Daisy means is that Emmy is gone."

"She left us a note saying that she had gone to help Santa," Daisy added. "Do you have any idea what she might mean?"

"Gone to help Santa!" the professor bellowed, setting his cup down hard on his desk. "What do you mean? WHAT SORT OF NONSENSE IS THIS?"

Jesse ducked as if the professor had hurled a snowball at him. "That's all she wrote," Jesse said in a meek whisper.

"We don't know any more than that," Daisy added. "Those are the bare facts."

"Well, the *bare facts,* young lady," said the professor, "are that you, her Keepers, whose job it is to look after her, left her out in the cold on Christmas Eve, and now you've got to find her and bring her back. I don't mind telling you that I have a *very bad* feeling about this. The base of operations for Santa Claus—aka Kris Kringle, aka St. Nicholas, aka Father Christmas—is the North Pole. But the North Pole has also been a veritable magnet for far less savory characters. You two had better get cracking if you—"

But before the professor could finish what he was saying, the screen of Jesse's old computer was swallowed up by a blizzard of static.

Jesse smacked the side of the monitor. It didn't help. Then he turned to Daisy. "Do you think Emmy might have decided to look for Santa by actually going to the North Pole?" he asked.

Daisy shook her head. "I don't know. And the only way we could get there to check would be by flying on Emmy's back."

They were just pondering this when the doorbell rang. Daisy dashed downstairs, Jesse at her heels.

They opened the door a crack and peered out. Miss Alodie was wearing a pair of fuzzy green earmuffs with a lumpy green scarf wrapped around her lower face and a long, fuzzy orange coat. She looked like a human carrot.

"Merry Christmas to all, and to all a good morning!" she cried out, her blue eyes dancing.

"Shh!" Jesse and Daisy said, pointing behind them up the stairs.

Miss Alodie nodded and whispered, "Oh! I see! The parents still nestled all snug in their beds, eh? Well, they're missing out, aren't they? Who could have imagined it? Yesterday it was fifty-five degrees and warm enough to make my crocuses consider poking their silly heads out of the dirt. Today we're walking in a winter wonderland!"

The twinkle in her blue eyes dimmed as they traveled shrewdly from Jesse to Daisy. "Why so glum on a snowy Christmas morn, kids?"

"Emmy's gone," said Jesse.

"Gone?" Miss Alodie echoed. "Gone where?"

"She said she went to help Santa," said Daisy. "We think she might have gotten it into her head to look for him at the North Pole, but we have no way to get there to find out."

"Well, in that case, my Christmas gifts to you are just the ticket," said Miss Alodie.

"The ticket?" Jesse asked.

"Your ticket to the North Pole!" she crowed. She turned and picked up two packages wrapped in purple tissue paper that had been sitting in the snow behind her. She handed them to Jesse and Daisy.

"Well," said Miss Alodie, "what are you waiting for? Unwrap them!"

Miss Alodie came inside and scraped the snow off her boots on the mat, then followed Daisy and Jesse into the living room. Unwrapping their gifts, Jesse and Daisy both made polite noises, but neither of them had the slightest idea what Miss Alodie had given them. Each of them held a pair of what looked like crude, short-handled badminton rackets made out of interwoven twigs and moss and lashed together with vines.

"They're *snowshoes!*" Miss Alodie said, slapping her thighs with elfin glee. "Made them myself from willow branches."

"Thanks a lot, Miss Alodie," Jesse said, but he was thinking that Miss Alodie's snowshoes didn't look as if they'd get them across the street, much less to the North Pole.

"Don't thank me," Miss Alodie said. "Just find your dragon and bring her back home safe and sound. I'll stick around here long enough to see you off and give your parents the most valuable gift any grown-up could ever wish for."

"What's that?" Jesse and Daisy both asked at once.

"Why, a long winter's nap, of course," she said with a wink. She pursed her lips and tapped her foot. "Now, let's see . . . you'll need to bring some snacks with you. It gets very cold at the North Pole and you'll be burning calories to stay warm."

Jesse and Daisy, humoring Miss Alodie, went to the kitchen. Neither of them thought for a minute that they were actually going to the North Pole. People who went on polar expeditions spent months preparing. They dressed like astronauts and ate special food made in high-tech labs.

Meanwhile, Jesse plugged in his Blueberry to recharge it. Wherever they were going, it wouldn't hurt to have access to the grid, as Uncle Joe liked to say.

"Do you think this is enough cocoa?" Jesse asked Daisy as he poured some into a thermos.

Daisy shrugged. Then her eyes suddenly lit up and she ran out of the room. Moments later, she came bounding back with her arms full of what looked like blue plastic pancakes.

"Thermal gel pads," she explained. "There's a chemical in them that makes them heat up. We can stuff them in our mittens and boots."

"You act like we're actually going to the North Pole," Jesse said.

Daisy shrugged again. "Can't hurt."

After Jesse and Daisy had filled the backpack with snacks, the thermal gel packs, the Blueberry, a flashlight, and one of Daisy's bandanas (for cold, runny noses), Miss Alodie helped them bundle up. Then she sat them down on the mudroom bench and fitted their feet into the snowshoes. The snowshoes might have looked crude but they slipped on over their boots as if they had been custom-made. Jesse stood up and almost fell over.

"Tsk, tsk. They work best in the snow," Miss

Alodie said, pushing them out the back door.

Jesse took a step off the back porch. Instead of sinking into the snow, he found himself standing on top of it. He slid his other foot forward and began to skate along the crest of the snow. He felt as if he were walking on water. It was smooth and effortless.

"These work great!" he said to Daisy.

"Let me try," Daisy said. She launched herself off the porch and landed as light as goose down beside Jesse. "Wow!" she said. "It's like we're weightless!"

They slid in a circle on top of the snow, whooping and waving their arms. Meanwhile, Miss Alodie was tapping on the mudroom window, pointing toward the laurel bushes.

"I think she wants us to head north," Jesse said. "Toward the barn."

Side by side, they glided up the backyard. It was like sliding over butter. Jesse almost believed they could slide all the way to the North Pole.

They came to the laurel bushes and fell forward, paddling on their bellies like penguins on an ice floe. When Jesse pulled himself through the last of the laurel bushes, he emerged into darkness so complete, he thought something had happened to his eyes.

Behind him, Daisy sucked in her breath. "Who turned out the lights?" she cried.

Jesse checked the illuminated face of his watch. It was ten o'clock in the morning, but it looked like midnight.

"Where's the barn, Jess?" Daisy said.

Squinting through the darkness, they could see that the barn was gone. The Dell was gone, the Deep Woods were gone, and when Jesse spun around to look for the laurel bushes, he discovered that they, too, were gone. In their place was an empty field of snow and ice.

"Look, Jesse!" Daisy said, her head tilted back.

The vast dome of the sky was blue-black and spangled with stars except for directly overhead, where red and green lights danced like a curtain made of twisted ropes, the fringed ends dangling tantalizingly just out of reach.

"It's the aurora borealis!" Jesse said.

"But it's right over our heads," Daisy said. "Not on the horizon like before."

"That's because we're at the North Pole, directly underneath them," Jesse said, suddenly understanding what had happened. "When Miss Alodie said these snowshoes were the ticket to the North Pole, she wasn't fooling around."

Daisy said, "If I'd known we were really coming

to the North Pole, I would have put on even more layers."

The air was dry and crisp. Their breath puffed out before them, but that was the only sign of cold. Jesse felt perfectly comfortable in what had to be subarctic temperatures.

"I don't think we need extra layers or gel packs or anything," he said. "I think the snowshoes not only got us here, they are keeping us warm, too."

The next moment, Daisy clutched at his sleeve. "Do you hear that?" she asked.

The air rang with a bright and cheery sound. At first he thought it was the wind, but as it grew louder, it became more musical.

"You know what that is, Jesse Tiger?" Daisy said, jumping up and down and flapping her mittened hands. "That's sleigh bells!"

CHAPTER THREE

BABES IN TOYLAND

The jingling sound grew louder until it filled the air. Daisy gasped as a team of reindeer with broad golden antlers came into view. Hitched two abreast by colorfully embroidered harnesses, they pulled a huge glossy black sleigh with golden runners that curled at the ends. Perched high up on the driver's seat was a figure so strikingly familiar that Daisy nearly laughed out loud.

As she stared at him, Daisy found herself mentally checking off the details: red suit trimmed with white fur, cheeks like roses, nose like a cherry, beard white as snow—except that he wasn't merry and lively and quick like the little man in the famous poem Jesse had been reading to Emmy. This man was big and hulking and serious-looking. As the sleigh bore down upon them, the driver pulled up on the reins and sat back. Then he burst into jolly laughter, his belly hanging over his low-slung black belt and jiggling like a bowl full of jelly.

"Ho-ho-ho, my wee little tykes! Welcome to the North Pole. You must be Emerald's Keepers!"

His voice was loud and deep and filled Daisy's head with a warm fuzzy feeling. Daisy groped for Jesse's hand. She didn't know whether to laugh or cry.

"Why the long faces, youngsters? She'll be happy to see you," Santa Claus went on. "It's a good thing I was out patrolling for my runaway reindeer."

Now that Santa mentioned it, Daisy noticed that there was an empty spot in one of the runners. The eighth reindeer. Daisy blinked back tears. It was true. It was all true. She turned to Jesse and said, "Jess, it's really him. It's not a myth after all! Santa Claus is *real!*"

Jesse nodded eagerly as he looked over the reindeer. "I wonder which one ran off."

"Look, Jess!" She pointed to the back of the sleigh to a compartment high up behind the driver's seat. Tucked beneath a red blanket with white fur trim were at least a dozen adorable little creatures with pointy noses and chins, upturned eyes, and green caps with bells on the ends.

"Santa's elves!" Jesse said. He turned to Daisy, his eyes as wide as hers.

"Hop in, my wee tykes, and I'll give you a lift," said Santa Claus. He held up a thick fur lap blanket. Jesse and Daisy scrambled into the bottom of the sleigh next to Santa's big black silver-buckled boots. Santa tucked the blanket around them. Daisy was overwhelmed by a feeling of coziness. She said to herself, *It's Christmas morning and here I am, tucked into Santa's sleigh!*

Just then, Santa snapped the reins and, as the sleigh started to move, called out the familiar string of names: "Now, Dasher! Now, Dancer! Now, Prancer and Vixen! On, Comet! On, Cupid! On, Donner!"

Daisy turned to Jesse and whispered, "There's your answer, Jess."

"That bad boy Blitzen," Jesse said with a shiver of excitement.

The sound of the harness bells and the warmth of the blanket made Daisy feel drowsy. She didn't want to fall asleep—she didn't want to miss a single moment of this adventure—but all of a sudden her eyelids were so heavy, she couldn't stay awake.

She woke to Jesse gently shaking her. Daisy rubbed her eyes and looked around. The sleigh had stopped. Reindeer hooves scraped restlessly on the ice and snow as Santa Claus heaved himself up and out of the sleigh.

"Oh, wow!" said Jesse, pointing.

Daisy saw not the cozy, quaint little snow-encrusted cottage featured in all the Santa's Villages she had ever visited, but a shimmering white palace with towers that seemed to scrape the sky. Looking at the sky, Daisy noticed something odd. It might have been an illusion created by the high towers, but the aurora borealis seemed to shine everywhere except where the palace stood.

"Welcome to my humble abode," said Santa. He clapped his hands, and the elves tumbled down off the back of the sleigh and scrambled onto each other's shoulders to reach the reindeer's harnesses. It took a team of four elves to wrestle the harness off each animal and lead it away.

Jesse stepped out of the sleigh and up the palace stairs. He ran his hands over the walls. "They're ice. Solid ice, Daisy," he said. He stood back and stared up at the palace. "The whole thing's made of ice."

Daisy joined him. Jesse was right. Every part of the palace—the walls, the roof, the window frames—was made of ice.

"Ice is the only building material here," Santa said as he stepped up to the big front door. It had a doorknob the size of a cantaloupe and required both of Santa's big gloved hands to turn. It opened with a loud creak, just like a wooden door.

Jesse and Daisy stepped into the vast entrance hall. In the center of the room was a life-sized ice sculpture of Santa Claus presenting a package to a small child. An icicle chandelier hanging from the domed ceiling seemed to sparkle from within. The slick ice walls glowed pale blue as if there were tubes of fluorescent light behind them. Twin grand staircases wound up to the right and left. An open door to the side offered Daisy a peek into a vast room in which there was a long table made of ice with a long ice bench on either side.

"Kindly remove your snowshoes, my wee little tykes," Santa said. "Mrs. Claus wouldn't want you to scuff up my nice ice floors!"

Jesse and Daisy consulted each other silently. The snowshoes had gotten them to the North Pole. Maybe now that they were under Santa's roof, they wouldn't need them. They untied the snowshoes and left them by the front door.

"This way," Santa said. Big boots jingling, Santa set off down a wide corridor.

Jesse and Daisy followed him. On the walls were ice carvings of candy canes and reindeer, one of them sporting a large bulbous nose.

"Rudolph," Daisy said to Jesse. Even inside the palace, her breath made plumes of condensation. Now that they'd taken off their snowshoes, she noticed that her feet, in her white fuzzy boots, had begun to grow numb from the cold. The walls and floor and ceiling of the corridor all glowed with the same pale blue of the entrance hall. If there was a light source, she thought, maybe there would be a heat source wherever Santa was leading them.

The corridor branched out like an icy maze, but Santa kept bearing left, leading them past more ice carvings of elves, swans, wreaths, garlands, and Christmas stockings. Daisy rubbed her hands together as they walked. Her fingertips were tingling from the cold. She looked over at Jesse. His teeth were chattering and his eyes, beneath his shaggy brown bangs, were watering.

Daisy gave her scarf an extra wrap around her lower face and reached over to do the same for Jesse. He flashed her a grateful look as Santa took another left turn at an ice statue of a snowman with a top hat, ice carrot nose, and ice pipe sticking out of its mouth.

"Frosty," Daisy said through her scarf. "Now I know how he feels."

"So far, I've counted sixty-three doors and fourteen staircases," Jesse said to her through his scarf. "I wonder where they lead."

"To toys?" Daisy asked. She didn't even play with toys anymore, but the thought that Santa's actual workshop was located somewhere in this building made her heart pirouette like a ballerina.

The hallway widened. In the center of the space was a sculpture of two happy children skating, their arms linked. Opposite the sculpture was a door. Santa opened the door and stood to one side. "I'll let you two wee tykes settle in. I think you'll find everything you need. Make yourselves at home."

"Can we see Emmy?" Jesse asked.

"In a bit. I've been keeping her busy," he said with a wink.

Daisy wondered how Santa was keeping Emmy busy. Using her flame to heat this place would be a good start. Jesse and Daisy stepped through the door, and Santa closed it behind them. They were standing in a sort of sitting room. Directly across from them were French windows. There were two doors on opposite sides of the room. Jesse opened each one.

"Bedrooms," he reported.

On one side of the sitting room was a huge carved wardrobe. On the other, two chairs stood before a fireplace in which flames licked the hearth. Daisy went over and huddled there. After a moment, she grumbled, "Ugh. This fire is *cold!*"

Jesse looked thoughtful. "Maybe real fire would melt this place. But Miss Alodie was right about how when you're cold you burn calories staying warm. I'm starved."

Jesse slung off the backpack and sat in one of the chairs, breaking out the trail mix and the thermos of cocoa. He looked over at Daisy. "Better hurry before I eat it all. Aren't you hungry?"

"I'm t-t-t-too cold to be hungry," said Daisy, shivering in front of the fake fire.

After a quick snack, Jesse zipped the trail mix bag closed and screwed the lid back on the thermos. Wiping his mouth on his sleeve, he wandered over to the windows.

"Is it still dark out?" Daisy asked.

"We're only a few days past the winter solstice," Jesse said, peering out the window. "This time of year at the North Pole, the sun never rises. It's dark twenty-four seven. And speaking of dark, come look at this!"

Daisy came to stand next to Jesse and looked out through the clear pane of ice. What was there to see? It was pitch dark outside. The aurora borealis shone some distance away, but not anywhere near where they were.

"Look down," Jesse said.

Daisy did and her head swam. The ice palace was perched on the edge of a precipice, plunging down into an abyss.

"We must be on top of a glacier," Jesse said.

Daisy backed away from the window and returned to the fireplace. Cozying up to a fake fire was better than staring into an abyss. Just when Daisy remembered the thermal gel pads in the backpack, Jesse said, "Maybe these will help."

He was standing before the open wardrobe. Daisy joined him. Hanging side by side were two identical green snowsuits lined with fur, with mittens attached to the sleeves. There were also two pairs of furry embroidered boots.

"What kind of fur is this, do you think?" Daisy asked, fingering the snowsuits.

"Rabbit," he guessed.

"Poor bunny," Daisy said. "And what are these boots made of?"

"Reindeer," Jesse said reluctantly. "I did a social studies unit last year on Laplanders. You know, the people who herd reindeer near the Arctic Circle. They prefer to be called Samis."

"I guess if this is good enough for Samis, it's good enough for us," said Daisy.

They took the snowsuits and boots into their bedrooms and changed. The moment Daisy put on the snowsuit, she was so flooded with warmth that she felt positively dizzy. She was standing next to a big ice bed with an ice canopy and a large fur quilt, and wondered whether it would be okay to lie down just for a few minutes, until the dizziness passed. She was about to test the "mattress" when she heard a familiar voice sing out: "Hello, Jesse Tiger! Hello, Daisy Flower! Welcome to Toyland! Toyland! Toyland! Dear little girl and boy land!"

Meanwhile, in his bedroom, Jesse had taken off his coat and was struggling to get his snowsuit on over his hoodie. As he fastened the little silver buttons up the front, he noticed that although the suit was a little tight—like something he had outgrown by several years—it made him feel cozy and warm.

"Thank you, Santa!" Jesse whispered. He felt a little dizzy, but he chalked it up to the sudden change in temperature. Then he got the raw emerald out of his coat pocket and transferred it to his snowsuit pocket.

By the time he came into the sitting room, Daisy was perched on Emmy's lap. Emmy was wearing a large green elf's cap with a silver bell dangling at the end. The top of the hat brushed the ceiling. She jingled it when she saw Jesse and gave him a roguish grin.

"Do you like my hat?" Emmy asked. "Santa gave it to me. I'm Santa's helper now. Didn't I tell you that Santa wasn't a myth?"

"You sure did," said Jesse giddily.

"How did you and Santa meet?" Daisy asked.

"He came to the barn last night, just as the snow was starting to fall, and picked me up in his sleigh," Emmy said. "He needs my help. Santa has been having trouble competing with the toy companies and all their fancy digital toys and computer games. He's asked me to help create a super-duper line of toys for girls and boys that will put Santa back on the map."

"That sounds great to me," said Jesse.

Emmy said, "He also asked me to get him a special present." She put a talon to her lips.

49

"Shhhhh. I haven't given it to him yet."

"What is it?" Jesse asked in a whisper.

"It's a secret," Emmy said, her eyes gleaming. "But I got it from the Time Before."

Jesse and Daisy exchanged puzzled looks. The Time Before? That was the mysterious place dragons came from.

"Wait till you hear about the fancy toys I'm designing," Emmy continued.

"What kind of toys?" Jesse asked.

"Well, for starters, I was thinking about action figures."

"Um, Em," Jesse said, "I hate to tell you this, but action figures have been around since my father was a kid. There's nothing fancy about them."

"Not *that* kind of action figures," Emmy said slyly. "This is actually more of a kit that kids can use to convert their boring old action figures into real-life action figures. Get it?"

"You mean," Jesse said slowly, "that my Superman action figure—"

"Could leap tall buildings and really and truly bend steel in his bare hands," Emmy said.

"Wow!" Jesse said.

"That's just the beginning," Emmy said. "I'm also thinking about a mask that will help kids shape-shift."

"You're kidding!" Daisy crowed, shaking her hands in excitement. "That's so cool!"

"And an invisibility suit!" Emmy said.

"Even better!" said Jesse, jumping up and down.

"But first, we have to get Santa's Toyland Vortex machine online and working," Emmy said.

"Toyland *Vortex machine*?" Jesse said. He wasn't sure he liked the sound of that.

Emmy nodded. "Santa already built it, but he needs me to operate it. Plus I'm helping him tweet it."

"Tweak it, you mean," Jesse said.

Emmy shrugged. "I tested it once by bringing in Santa's special present. Before long it will produce all the magical toys I'm dreaming up."

"When can we see it?" Daisy asked.

"Soon. It's outside. But first let me show you around inside. You two have a treat in store!"

Emmy led the way out the door and down the hall, to a set of wide, arched doors with crossed candy canes carved into them. "Wait till you get a load of this," she said as she pushed the doors open.

Inside, the room hustled and bustled with hundreds of elves seated at painted wooden benches, all of them hard at work. Each long bench functioned as a kind of mini assembly line. At the nearest bench, the first elf carved a piece of wood until it resembled the hull and cabin of a ship. The second elf sanded it. The third painted it. The fourth threaded ropes through the tiny deck rail, then handed it off to the elves at the next bench, who were busily carving and sanding and painting tiny wooden animals, two by two.

"It's Noah's ark!" Jesse cried. "I had one just like that."

"Would you like to have another one?" Emmy asked.

Jesse nodded eagerly. He knew he was way too old to play with a Noah's ark set. And yet he wanted that toy so badly, his fingers, in their furry mittens, itched to play with it! Perhaps it was the thrill of knowing it had come straight from Santa's workshop. Perhaps it was the shiny painted animals, two by two, exactly like the ones he had lined up so carefully on the blue wooden ramp of his own ark for hours at a time.

Meanwhile, Daisy was gazing at a doll with yellow yarn hair and bright blue button eyes. The pattern on her dress was little daisies. Over the dress she wore a starched white pinafore. The elf working on the doll noticed and handed it to Daisy.

"It's Flower, Jess!" Daisy said, hugging the doll. "Remember?"

How could Jesse forget? Daisy had gotten

Flower the same Christmas Jesse had gotten Noah's ark, the Christmas he and his parents had spent at Daisy's house. He and Daisy had been six years old.

At the next series of benches, the elves were making cars and trucks and all sorts of things that go. Jesse was given a little blue biplane and Daisy a bright red fire truck with a shiny metal ladder.

At each area of the workshop they came to, the elves seemed to sense which toys appealed to them and offered them up, so shiny and fresh they even *smelled* new. Jesse and Daisy, eyes aglitter, held out their arms and accepted the gifts with shameless glee. After all, it was Christmas and here they were, at the source of Christmas joy, Santa's very own workshop!

By the time the cousins had completed their tour, they were loaded down with toys. When their arms could hold no more, one of the elves followed along behind them pulling a miniature sled piled high with their goodies.

They arrived back at the front door to find Santa waiting for them, a big, jolly smile on his face.

"Thank you, Santa!" Jesse and Daisy chirped.

"Ho-ho-ho! It's my pleasure! But next Christmas, make way for Emerald's super-duper new line of toys!" Santa boomed.

Jesse nodded, but in a way, there was something about the simple gifts he and Daisy had received that seemed just right for Christmas. Did Christmas even really *need* Emmy's magic? Wasn't Christmas magic enough all by itself?

Santa Claus turned to Emmy, a big smile wreathing his face. "And where is *my* Christmas present, Miss Emerald?"

Emmy said, "Hidden away someplace where you can't find it, Mister Santa."

He frowned in disappointment. "Oh. But it's Christmas Day. Everyone else in the world has already gotten their presents. Can't I have mine?"

The cousins listened to this strange exchange with open mouths.

"Have you been a good little boy all year?" Emmy asked.

"I've been as good as good can be," said Santa Claus. "And I want my present. You promised." He pouted.

"Did I? Well, maybe after dinner," said Emmy. "And only if you're very good. Right now, I don't know about my two Keepers here, but I'm *starving*!"

CHAPTER FOUR

THE CLAUS

Santa's Great Hall was the same room they had
seen when they first entered the palace. It was the
size of a school gym, with a table in the middle that
was as long as a bowling alley. A row of dark windows lined one wall, with a long carved sideboard

running underneath it. An icicle chandelier hung over the table, beaming down the same cold blue light that illuminated the rest of the palace. Something about the light was beginning to bother Jesse. He missed the buttery warmth of the sunlight.

Santa had excused himself after they left the workshop and gone to his room to change. When Emmy, Jesse, and Daisy entered the Great Hall, they found him sitting at the head of the long table. Instead of his traditional suit, he wore a red embroidered smoking jacket with a green ascot tucked into the collar. He was smoking a long black pipe that was as thin as a cigarette. While he still looked like Santa, he looked like Santa taking a break.

Jesse didn't want to say anything, but Santa's pipe made him wonder: *Shouldn't the North Pole be a smoke-free zone?*

Emmy seated Daisy in the middle of the bench on one side of the table, and then Jesse right across from her. When Emmy sat down at the foot of the table, Santa lifted a small silver bell and rang it.

A dozen elves in white aprons streamed into the Great Hall bearing platters.

Jesse's stomach rumbled. He licked his lips and picked up his ice fork and his ice knife.

Across the table, Daisy said, "I'm ravenous, Jess, aren't you?"

"Am I ever!" said Jesse, his eyes following the progress of the platters.

"I wonder what we're having," Daisy said.

Jesse couldn't wait to find out. The elves served Santa first. After Santa had piled his plate high with what looked like a mixed grill of meats and fish, the elves moved around to Daisy. Daisy looked at what the elves were offering and hesitated.

"Just take some of everything," Jesse whispered. "If you can't eat it, I will."

Jesse had never been this hungry in his life. He watched Daisy take her ice fork and spear a piece of meat onto her plate, then another, and another, taking time to select each piece. *Speed it up, Daise,* Jesse urged her silently.

Daisy said "Thank you" to the elves. The elves nodded, then went to Emmy, who helped herself to hearty portions of everything.

Jesse's stomach kicked up such a ruckus, he actually felt as if he were having a hunger attack. Suddenly, he couldn't wait another moment. He reached between the buttons of his snowsuit into his hoodie pouch, where he had stashed Aunt Maggie's sesame cracker with goat cheese. He pulled it out and bit into it.

Sweet relief!

Then he nearly choked.

He looked down. Instead of Aunt Maggie's sesame cracker, he'd mistakenly grabbed Miss Alodie's blue goo cracker. It tasted weird, but he didn't want to spit it out. He chewed quickly, swallowed, and tucked the rest of the cracker back in his hoodie pouch.

Something very curious happened next. Not only did his growling stomach calm down, but he was no longer in the least bit hungry. He felt as if he had just devoured an entire banquet. By the time the serving elves got around to Jesse, the thought of eating another bite actually filled him with revulsion.

For appearances' sake, Jesse loaded up his plate with three kinds of meat and two kinds of fish.

"Ho-ho-ho! Eat up, tykes," Santa boomed from the head of the table.

"What are we eating?" Jesse asked, trying to make polite conversation.

"We have fillets of baby dolphin with krill sauce, sirloin of seal pup, grizzly bear cub cheeks, and caribou calf steak . . . bloody rare."

Jesse shuddered in disgust. *No thank you, Santa!*

Meanwhile, across the table, Jesse was shocked to see Daisy shoveling food into her mouth. Daisy was practically a vegetarian. She didn't even like to eat hamburgers, much less baby anything, including baby corn!

"Psst, Daisy!" Jesse called across to her.

Daisy looked up, her eyes strangely glassy. She gave him a grouchy frown and growled, "I am eating. Go away and don't bother me."

"Well, excuse me," Jesse said. He looked over at Emmy. She had the same intent, glassy-eyed look as she devoured the food on her plate. Emmy ate meat, but she had a soft spot for babies of any species. She would never in her right mind have eaten them for dinner.

Something fishy was going on. Were both Emmy and Daisy, stuffing their faces with this all-you-can-eat baby-animal buffet, under some sort of spell to which Miss Alodie's cracker had made him resistant? He couldn't know for certain, but one thing he did know: he was not going to touch one bite of his dinner. He began to cut up his food and move it, piece by piece, down onto the bench next to him and, from there, onto the floor beneath the table. While he did this, he listened with one ear to the conversation Santa and Emmy were having across the length of the table.

"I want you to file down the cogs on the re-uptake inhibitor so it will function more smoothly," Santa was saying. He leaned back from the table.

He was picking his teeth with a fishbone. The beard around his mouth was stained yellow.

"Will do," said Emmy in an unfamiliar droning voice. "I will see to it forthwith. We will have to suction out the particles. Otherwise they will clog the works and make the carburetor malfunction."

"We must avoid that," Santa said. "And another thing we need to look at is the insulation in the cooling chamber."

"I will take care of that, as you wish, Claus," Emmy said, her green eyes wide and empty.

The tone of her voice and the look in her eyes bothered Jesse. Besides which, Emmy was a magical dragon. She had never shown much aptitude for machines. Did this mysterious new mechanical ability come with whatever spell she was under? And *Claus*? What was going on?

As Jesse listened, he fiddled with the raw emerald in his snowsuit pocket. A question popped into his head, and before he realized he was interrupting, he blurted it out: "Where's *Mrs.* Claus?"

Santa stopped midsentence and tugged at his mustache.

"Hush," said Daisy, frowning deeply, her mouth full of food. "You are a rude little boy."

Jesse wanted to tell her that speaking with her mouth full made her a rude little girl, but Emmy said, "He poses an excellent question. Where is she? I would like to meet this fabled personage."

Santa leaned forward and whispered, "Don't let this get out, but Mrs. Santa is down at the Honolulu Hilton, in her polka-dot bikini, basking in the sunshine."

"Goody for her," Daisy said in a flat voice.

"Really? Hawaii?" said Jesse to Santa. It was hard to imagine the plump, apple-cheeked Mrs. Claus wearing a bikini, polka-dotted or otherwise.

Santa and Emmy had resumed their discussion of thermonuclear turbines when a more important question occurred to Jesse. "Why do you need our dragon's help again?"

Santa turned an icy blue gaze upon Jesse. "I have need of her dragon magic."

"Yeah, but don't you have Santa magic of your own?" he asked.

Daisy, her cheeks stuffed with food, growled at Jesse: "Leave the Claus alone. Eat up and shut up."

Daisy never said "Shut up." Ever. The elves came by to offer seconds. Jesse held up his hands and said, "I'm good." But he wasn't good. He was worried sick. Both Emmy and Daisy were suddenly strangers to him.

As an elf leaned in to take his empty plate, Jesse got a whiff of something rank. Rotting fish?

Where had that come from? He'd been near the elves before, when they were unhooking the reindeer from their traces, and he hadn't noticed any particular scent then, much less something this gross. Were the elves not entirely what they seemed?

"Well!" said Santa, pushing back from the table and resting his hands on his belly. "Now that we've all eaten our fill, I think it's time to get down to business."

Santa Claus rang the little silver bell again. Two elves marched in carrying a large scroll, a quill, and a small bottle of ink.

"I want to thank you two for coming all this way," he said to Jesse and Daisy. "Had you not come to me, I would most certainly have had to come to you. I have a proposition to make."

"We are always open to a proposition from the Claus!" Daisy droned. She set down her fork, having cleaned her plate for the third time. Her cheeks were pink and greasy, her eyes glassy.

Jesse turned to Santa. "What's the proposition?"

Santa leaned forward. "I stand ready to give you a bounty of toys—more toys than you ever imagined, two each of every toy I have ever made—if you will sign over the Keepership of Emerald the Dragon to me. I have taken the liberty of having a document drawn up."

"Toys are us!" Daisy chanted. "We want more toys! More, more, more!"

Jesse didn't know what astonished him more, Santa's business proposition or Daisy's reaction to it. He sputtered, "Are you crazy?"

Santa turned to Jesse. His eyes narrowed to icy slivers, and he rasped, "Far from it, my lad." Then, snapping his fingers, he bid the elves to unfurl the scroll.

"Here is the contract for transference of title," Santa announced. "I trust you will find everything in order."

Jesse whipped around to Emmy. "You can't possibly want to go along with this, Em."

She gave him that disturbingly empty look and said, "We must not thwart the Claus."

"The Claus must be obeyed," droned Daisy. Her head swiveled toward the elves. "Bring the contract of the Claus! We are ready to sign for the Claus! The Claus rules!"

Jesse couldn't believe it. Was everybody nuts but him? "Wait a minute," he said, his voice rising in panic. "We need to discuss this first."

The elves, ignoring him, marched over to Daisy. Jesse got up on his knees and crawled halfway across the table to get a look at the contract. It was printed on old parchment paper. Jesse didn't recognize the language. He didn't even recognize the alphabet. It looked like bird tracks, lots of sharp wedges and triangles.

Just then, Jesse felt something pulse in his snowsuit pocket, like a cell phone set to vibrate. The emerald! He reached in and pulled it out.

Meanwhile, one of the elves handed the quill to Daisy.

"Show me where to sign," Daisy said in the dead, singsong voice.

Jesse opened his hand and looked at the stone. It was as clear as glass; the emerald's natural green color had completely disappeared. He was in the presence of treachery. Something was rotten at the North Pole!

CHAPTER FIVE

THE BAD MAN CAVE

Daisy touched the point of the quill to the document.

Jesse dived the rest of the way across the table and landed on the bench beside her. Daisy frowned and slapped at him, as if he were a giant gnat.

"Let's take this back to the room and discuss it first," Jesse said. "After all, this is a big decision."

"We disobey the Claus at our own peril," Daisy said darkly.

"I'm sure 'the Claus' will understand our need to discuss this first." Jesse plucked the quill from her fingers. He thrust it at an elf. To Santa, he said, "We're taking this contract back to our rooms with us. We'd like to discuss it. Does the Claus mind?"

Santa's blue eyes scorched him like dry ice. It was as if someone had stuck a pin in Santa. Beneath the smoking jacket, his jolly girth had dwindled down to nothing but muscle and sinew. "He minds very much. You disappoint me, boy. Know that my offer is good until midnight."

"Toys are us," Daisy chanted again, beating on the bench with her greasy fists. "We want toys!"

"We have all the toys we need, Daise," Jesse said between clenched teeth. "But can we save this discussion for when we're alone?"

Santa barked at the elves. "Escort them to their room. Let them take the contract with them as well as the quill and the bottle of ink. Know this: in the end, I will be obeyed." Santa gave Jesse a frigid look. His cheeks, which earlier had been rosy and plump, were now sunken and chiseled.

"Merry Christmas to you, too," Jesse muttered. Gone were the twinkly eyes, the dimply cheeks, the nose like a cherry, the mouth like a bow, and the jolly belly that shook like a bowl full of jelly. The man he was looking at might have a white beard, but that was where the resemblance to jolly old Saint Nick ended. The blue goo cracker had not only protected Jesse from the food, which he was now convinced had put a spell on Emmy and Daisy, but it had also undone a masking spell and revealed their host to be someone other than Santa Claus.

Jesse turned to Emmy. "Can you come with us? This concerns you, too."

Emmy said, "I must stay with the Claus and serve him."

"Right." Jesse sighed and shook his head in disgust.

Two elves rolled up the contract and led the way back to Jesse and Daisy's suite. Beside him, Daisy walked stiffly, like a robot. But Jesse's attention was on the elves. With every step, their elfin escort was undergoing a transformation. Their delicate little feet broke out of their slippers and sprouted dusty gray fur and claws. Their shoulders broadened, and huge humps appeared on their backs. They swayed along like chimpanzees.

Jesse didn't know what they were, but they

weren't elves and never had been, any more than their host was Santa Claus.

The sculptures in the hallway began to transform, too. The cheerful Christmas-themed characters gave way to a terrifying gallery featuring giant bears, fierce wolves, slithering serpents, warriors with horned helmets, grimacing trolls, and other creatures Jesse didn't even have names for.

When their escort turned to usher Jesse and Daisy into their room, Jesse stared at their faces in numb horror. Their eyes, no longer delicate and upturned, were now huge and goggly, poking out of the tops of their scabby foreheads. Their jaws hung open nearly to the floor, revealing jagged yellow fangs. The rotten fish odor he'd smelled before had become overpowering.

Jesse looked at Daisy, but it was obvious from the expression on her face that all she saw were Santa's elves.

"I'll take those," Jesse said, plucking the scroll, quill, and ink bottle from the monsters' clutches. He went inside and set everything on the sitting room table. The monsters slammed the door behind them. When the sound of their claws dragging along the icy corridor faded away into silence, Jesse turned to Daisy and said, "Ready for your dessert?"

She frowned, but she licked her lips in antici-
pation. "What dessert?"

"It's a surprise," Jesse said. He reached into the
pouch of his sweatshirt and drew out the remains
of the blue goo cracker. "The Claus himself had it
prepared for you." He broke the cracker in half and
returned the last quarter to his pouch.

"Open your mouth and close your eyes, and I'll
give you something to make you wise," he said.
Daisy shut her eyes and stuck out her tongue. Jesse
placed the cracker piece in her mouth and said,
"Chew and swallow."

Daisy's eyes fluttered open in suspicion as she
chewed. "Hey," she said sharply. She swallowed and
said, "How dare you . . . ?" Then, as Jesse watched,
Daisy's face turned an alarming shade of purple.
Her eyes widened and she clapped a hand over her
mouth.

"Jess! I'm going to be sick!" she gasped.

Dragging her across the room, he flung the
French windows open and held on to her as she
spewed up what looked like the entire lumberjack
buffet into the abyss.

When she was finished, he pulled her back in,
shut the window, and sat her down on one of the
ice chairs.

"Better?" Jesse asked.

Daisy nodded weakly. Her eyes were clear, but she looked as pale as chalk. "What happened?" she asked.

Jesse took a deep breath. "I think we have been the victims of a masking spell cast by our host, who is *not* Santa. I think the food you ate was bewitched. I think he did that to force us to sign over Emmy to him. Miss Alodie's blue goo cracker, which you just ate—and which I ate by mistake before dinner—not only counteracted the bewitched food, but it seems to be undoing the masking spell."

Then he told Daisy how the emerald had revealed the presence of treachery. He told her how, not long after he ate Miss Alodie's cracker, the elves had started turning into something hideous.

"What did they look like?" Daisy asked.

Jesse described them.

"Trolls," Daisy said. "I saw a picture of them in a book in Alodie's Alley. They're ugly customers." She put a hand to her mouth. "Jess, remember what the professor said? The North Pole has been a magnet for unsavory characters."

"Whoever is pretending to be Santa seems pretty unsavory to me," Jesse said.

Daisy nodded slowly. "I remember, when I first heard the sleigh bells . . . they made me feel a little bit dizzy. I thought I was just overjoyed to be meeting Santa, but maybe . . ."

"The masking spell must have kicked in then," Jesse said.

"And when I climbed into the sled, I felt even dizzier." She reached out and grabbed his hand. "Jesse, we've been under his power ever since we got here!"

"A masking spell, for sure," Jesse said. "But we must not have been enough under his power to sign the contract. That's why he spelled the food. You might not have noticed it, but Emmy ate it, too, and she was as willing as you were to go along with the Claus's plan."

"Don't call him that," Daisy said.

"What should we call him?" Jesse said.

"Until we have a name, Mr. Unsavory will do," Daisy said. "And the question is, what does Mr. Unsavory want with our dragon?"

"I don't know," said Jesse. "Maybe it has to do with that Toyland Vortex machine Emmy's supposed to operate for him. Or whatever it is that Mr. Unsavory asked Emmy to give him from the Time Before. For whatever purpose he wants her, we stand a better chance against him if Emmy's no longer under his power."

"The blue goo cracker!" Daisy said. "Do you have any left?"

Jesse patted his hoodie pocket through his snowsuit. "Just enough for Emmy, I hope."

"Excellent!" said Daisy. "Let's find Emmy so we can feed her some blue goo."

"First," said Jesse, "I think we should take off these snowsuits."

Daisy looked surprised. "Really? But they're so warm," she said.

"If the food's bewitched, it stands to reason that the suits are, too. Don't you remember feeling just a little bit more fuzzy-headed as soon as you put it on?" Jesse asked.

"Now that you mention it . . ." Daisy immediately began taking off her snowsuit, as did Jesse. Stripping down to their street clothes, they raced to put on their coats and mittens and scarves and boots. They were still so cold, they hopped around and slapped themselves.

"I think we need those gel pads now!" Daisy cried. She pranced over to the backpack and got the pads. They were stiff, but when Daisy cracked them over her knee, they got soft and squishy and started to heat up. The cousins stuffed them into their sleeves and pant legs and boots, anywhere they would fit. They immediately felt spots of warmth wherever they had placed the pads. When they were finished, they were still cold, but at least they weren't freezing.

"Okay," Daisy said. "Where do we start to look for Emmy?"

"Before we do that, let's look over the contract and see if we can figure out who Mr. Unsavory is," said Jesse. "It would help to know who we're up against."

"Plan!" said Daisy.

They unrolled the contract and spread it out on the table. Because their and Emmy's names weren't written in the bird track language, they were able to pick them out. But they couldn't find any hint as to the identity of their host.

"What language is this, anyway?" Daisy asked.

"Beats me, but let's see if Blueberry Sal knows," said Jesse. "My mom said it has a really neat translation program. She uses it all the time in Africa."

Jesse got the Blueberry out of the backpack and peeled off his mittens. With his thumbs, he called up the translation program. Then he scanned the first line of the contract into the machine.

"Hmm," Jesse said. "Sal says the language is Old Norse. This first line says, 'The Keepers of the Dragon Emerald, being of sound mind and body . . .'"

"What's Old Norse?" Daisy asked.

Jesse looked at the Blueberry screen. "It says that it's an ancient Norwegian language that isn't used anymore," Jesse said.

"How weird is that?" said Daisy.

"Very," Jesse said. He looked Daisy in the eye. "I think we should destroy the contract."

"Really?" Daisy said, shocked. Destroying property, even if it belonged to Mr. Unsavory, bothered her.

"Sooner or later, he's going to catch us in a spell and make us sign it," Jesse said.

"And if we sign it, we lose Emmy," Daisy said.

She picked up the contract and tried to rip it in half, but the paper wouldn't tear.

"If we can't rip it," Jesse said, "we can ruin it." He unscrewed the lid on the ink bottle and splashed ink all over the contract. But the ink beaded up and dripped harmlessly to the floor. Jesse replaced the lid on the bottle and shook his head, perplexed.

"Fire!" Daisy exploded. "Fire's practically magical all by itself. We'll burn it."

She ran over and tossed the contract into the fireplace.

"The fire's fake, remember?" Jesse called after her.

The scroll churned around in the flames like a

piece of laundry in a washing machine. The next moment, it wafted out onto the floor.

"Grrrr," Daisy said. She took the contract, wadded it up into a tight little ball, and flung it back into the flames. But once again, the contract smoothed itself and floated out of the fire.

"I am so sick of this lame flame!" Daisy said.

"Give up, Daisy," Jesse said, pacing between the wardrobe and the fireplace.

Daisy pulled the mitten off one hand and passed her bare hand through the fire. She felt nothing. She stuck her hand in and held it there. She still felt nothing. But while her hand was in the flames, the fire began to make a noise. It wasn't a crackly fire kind of noise. It was more musical than that. It sounded like icicles melting, each drop a different note.

"Hey, Jess?" Daisy said, staring at the colorful flames in fascination. She suddenly realized that they were red and green—just like the aurora borealis! Daisy remembered Emmy sitting up on the barn roof, insisting that the northern lights were calling out to her with a message she couldn't quite understand. Were the lights in the sky and the lights in this fireplace somehow connected? And if so, were they trying to tell them something? "I think this fire might be trying to communicate with me."

"Ignore it. It's probably spelled, like everything else in this place," Jesse said. "We need to stop messing around and find some fire that really burns."

Daisy nodded. "There's got to be real fire some-place in this palace," she said, heading for the door. "And maybe while we're looking for that, we'll find Emmy, too."

"Wait," said Jesse. He shoved the scroll, quill, and ink bottle into the backpack, then followed her through the door.

The first thing they saw out in the corridor was an ice sculpture of a two-headed monster. It looked like a giant mutated horned toad.

"Ugh!" Daisy clapped a hand over her mouth. "What happened to the happy ice skaters?"

"I forgot to tell you," Jesse said. "Another result of lifting the masking spell is that all the cheery Christmas ice sculptures are now kind of scary."

Daisy nodded warily and skirted the monster. They proceeded down the hallway in the opposite direction of the main entrance. The next sculpture they encountered was a sea serpent with its tail coiled around a boat. Inside the boat was a bearded man with a horned helmet wielding a heavy sword.

"That looks like a Viking warrior," Jesse said, "which makes sense. Viking warriors come from

Norway, and Mr. Unsavory's contract is in Old Norse."

"And trolls come from Norway, too," Daisy added.

They continued down the corridor, passing ice sculptures of trolls swinging battle-axes and gnawing on bones. After a while, Daisy averted her eyes from the gruesome displays. But when they passed the ice sculpture of a giant hunchbacked monster with horns and fangs, holding a Viking warrior in his clawed fist, Daisy couldn't help but stare. "*That* thing is terrifying."

"It is, isn't it? It looks a lot like how I imagine Grendel," Jesse said.

"If that's Grendel," Daisy said with a snort, "I'd hate to see Hansel. Who's Grendel?"

"He's a monster that menaced the people of ancient Norway until a hero named Beowulf slew him," Jesse said. "It's a famous ancient Norse legend that took place a long time ago. Sometime in the eighth or ninth century, I think."

As they continued down the hall, they stopped at each door and tried the doorknob. All of them were locked. Finally, they came upon a giant door that had something very familiar about it.

"Well, now," Jesse said. "Isn't this a sight for sore eyes?" Carved into the ice above the door was a very lifelike sculpture of Emmy's head.

"This must be Emmy's room," said Daisy.

They knocked on the door but weren't surprised when there was no answer. They turned the knob and found it was also locked. "Still off serving the Claus," Jesse muttered.

"I guess we'll give her the blue goo later," Daisy said.

They continued until they arrived at a wide dead end. A set of doors loomed before them. Two wolves carved out of ice crouched on either side of the doors, ready to spring. One of them had a bone in its mouth. Daisy expected the wolves to leap forward and have her for lunch. She had to keep reminding herself that they were ice.

Jesse turned the knob. The door was locked.

"Surprise, surprise," Daisy said dully.

Jesse put an eye to the rather large keyhole and peered inside while Daisy stared at the wolf with the bone in its mouth. The words *skeleton key* popped into her head. On a hunch, she reached into the wolf's mouth and removed the bone.

The wolf's jaws snapped shut in a puff of cold smoke. Daisy looked at the bone. Carved into the end that had been hidden inside the wolf's mouth was a crude key.

She held it up to Jesse. He grinned as he took

the key from her, slid it into the keyhole, and turned it.

There was a clicking sound, and the door swung open.

Jesse stepped inside. Daisy, heart hammering, followed. The door closed behind them with another click.

It was an office. Though the walls and floor and ceiling were made of ice like everything else in the palace, the furniture was real. There was a big wooden desk with six drawers and a hefty leather-upholstered chair, a leather blotter on the desk with a neat stack of stationery, and a mug filled with pens. There was a drafting table and bookshelves filled with ancient leather-bound volumes. Photographs hung on the walls showed a hulking, broad-shouldered man with long white-blond hair, a neatly trimmed white beard, and chiseled features. He wore a dark business suit and was shaking hands with important-looking men and women. In all the pictures, he stood a head taller than everyone else.

Daisy and Jesse stared at the pictures. Jesse said, "Could that be . . . ?"

"Mr. Unsavory?" Daisy finished.

"It is!" Jesse said, looking closer. "I'd know those deep-freeze eyes anywhere. And if that's him, then this is his man cave."

"What's a man cave?" Daisy asked.

"A place a man goes to be alone and do his own thing. My mom says a man cave tells a lot about the man . . . his desk especially. If we're lucky, maybe we'll find out who Mr. Unsavory really is. If we're *really* lucky, maybe he keeps matches in his desk."

Daisy wandered over to the drafting table, and Jessie started looking through the desk. He picked up a piece of paper and held it out to Daisy. "Does the name Wolf ring any bells for you?" he asked.

"Nope," Daisy said. She was looking at another sheet of paper taped to the drafting table. It was a diagram of the earth with something poking out of the North Pole that looked like a giant tower or scaffold surrounded by swirly marks coming down from space. Other bits of paper tacked here and there were variations of the same design.

She called Jesse over. He cocked his head at the diagram. "I'll bet that's the Toyland Vortex machine Emmy mentioned. She didn't say it was sitting directly on top of the North Pole. It looks like a plan for a giant oil rig."

"Then Mr. Unsavory is an *oil tycoon*?" Daisy said. "Instead of a toy-making machine, Emmy's helping to build an oil rig?"

Jesse thought about this and then shook his head. "Plenty of people drill for oil in the Arctic and they don't need dragon magic to do it."

Daisy moved over to the shelves and started examining the books. "These look like they're all in Old Norse," she said. "Maybe Mr. Unsavory is a professor of Old Norse."

Jesse followed her and ran his fingers along the spines. "This one is in English," he said, pulling a volume down off the shelf. "What do you know? It's *Beowulf*."

"The Norse hero who slew Grendel?" Daisy asked, just as the section of bookcase Jesse had taken the volume from swung inward.

"Whoa!" Daisy said, pulling back. A passageway yawned before them. "Should we go in? I mean, what if he comes?"

"Let's chance it," Jesse said. "We still need to find matches. There weren't any in his desk."

Gingerly, they stepped through the small passageway into the room beyond. This room was nearly twice as big as the man cave, with a soaring vaulted ceiling made of ice. Medieval weapons hung from hooks and spikes pounded into the ice walls. There were broadswords and battle-axes and shields as tall as a grown man.

"You know what this is, don't you?" Jesse said in a voice filled with awe. "This is the *bad man* cave."

Daisy felt a chill work its way up her spine.

Numbly, she watched Jesse walk past the weapons, examining them without touching them. "I saw stuff like this in the British Museum," he said. "Definitely Viking. The Vikings were fierce warriors."

In the center of the room stood a seven-foot-tall ice mannequin clad in armor—a golden helmet and a fearsome suit of mail. Jesse, still carrying the book from the other room, said, "The trolls, the ice sculptures, the Old Norse, the armor . . . it all adds up."

"Adds up to what, Jess?" Daisy asked.

Jesse didn't answer. Against one wall stood a stout wooden barrel. He turned the tap and a stream of golden liquid poured out. Jesse dipped his finger in the stream and tasted it. "It's mead, Daisy," he said. "It's a beverage made from fermented water and honey. It was the drink of choice of the Viking horde."

"How come you're such an expert on Vikings?" Daisy asked.

"One of my parents' friends in Doctors Without Borders was Norwegian, and he—"

Jesse didn't finish. Something caught his eye, and he darted toward a table that looked like a museum display of household items. Among them was a primitive-looking meal kit: metal pot, cup, fork, spoon, and a small metal box shaped like a cylinder.

"Eureka," said Jesse, holding up the cylinder. Attached to the box by a chain was a D-shaped metal ring.

"What is it?" Daisy asked.

"It's a tinderbox," Jesse said. "This is how people started fires before matches were invented."

Jesse opened the top of the cylinder and up-ended it. A small rock fell out into the palm of his hand. Inside the cylinder, Daisy caught sight of a wick.

"This little rock is flint," Jesse said. "You take the flint and strike it against the metal ring and you get a spark. This wick inside the box is soaked in oil. The spark from the flint lights the wick inside the box, and presto, you've got fire."

"Okay, so how come you know so much about tinderboxes?" Daisy asked.

"Some people in Africa don't have matches," Jesse said. "They still use tinderboxes. This kid I used to play with in Tanzania, he taught me how to use his."

"Great. So let's fire it up and burn the contract," Daisy said.

"Right, but not here," said Jesse. "Let's go to Emmy's room. Maybe she's back. We can give her the blue goo *and* burn the contract. Once the spell is broken, she'll know that the man she's working for isn't Santa Claus."

"Yeah, but we still don't know who he really is," Daisy said.

"We do now," Jesse said solemnly. He walked Daisy back through the secret passageway. As he returned the book to the shelf, the passage sealed shut. Then he led her over to the desk and pointed at the inscription on the piece of paper he had held up earlier.

Daisy read it aloud. *From the desk of B. O. Wolf,*" she said. "I don't get it."

"*B. O. Wolf,*" Jesse said. "Ignore how it's written and listen to how it sounds."

"B-o-wolf," Daisy said slowly. "You mean . . . Beowulf? You think Mr. Unsavory is the guy who killed Grendel in that famous story you told me about? But that's just a story, Jesse! Besides, didn't you say it took place in the eighth or ninth century? Even if Beowulf was real, he couldn't be alive now!"

"But Beowulf's killing Grendel isn't the whole story," Jesse said. "Ten years after he did that and became king, he slew . . . a dragon."

"Oh, no!" Daisy sat down hard on the desk chair. "A dragon?"

Jesse nodded. "Supposedly Beowulf died after the battle. But now I'm thinking that Beowulf survived, faked the funeral, and hid the truth from the world, substituting the legend we've all learned. What he actually did was drink the blood of the dragon he slew. Like St. George, he achieved immortality."

Daisy shook her head. "Jesse Tiger, do you mean Mr. Unsavory, the guy who wants to be Emmy's new Keeper, is a *dragon slayer*?"

CHAPTER SIX

THE VORTEX INTERCEPTOR

When Emmy greeted Jesse and Daisy at the door to her room, they saw that her eyes burned feverishly. She was in desperate need of Miss Alodie's blue goo cracker.

Jesse and Daisy exchanged a worried look. On

their way from the man cave, they had discussed strategy. They knew all too well, from the day Emmy had been born, how difficult it was to get her to eat something when she didn't like the taste. Miss Alodie's blue goo cracker tasted nasty. Emmy might even spit it out, and they couldn't risk that. They'd decided they would use the distraction of burning the contract to get her to eat the cracker.

"I was having cookies and milk," Emmy droned. "Do come in."

Emmy turned, walked back into the room, and hunkered down in a giant easy chair carved to accommodate her draconic dimensions. A second chair, a table, and the fireplace were similarly large. On the table, there was a plate of cookies, each one the size of a cake. Also on the table were the other two pieces of Emmy's Christmas stationery.

Emmy gestured to the chair across from her. The layout of the room was identical to Jesse and Daisy's, except for its dragon scale, which made the cousins feel that much smaller and more helpless. The cousins climbed up into the second chair. It was big enough to fit both of them and about five other kids, too.

"Won't you have some?" Emmy asked, gesturing at the cake-sized cookies.

"No, thanks," said Daisy. "We're here on other

business. We're here to burn the contract, because we have no intention of giving you up to the Claus."

Emmy shook her head rapidly. "The Claus will be very angry with you."

Jesse jumped down from the chair and shrugged off his backpack. He took out the scroll and held it up to her. "Too bad. We're burning it anyway."

"Me and my precious flame will not be a party to this wanton destruction," Emmy said, clamping her talons over her snout.

"It just so happens we don't need you or your precious flame," Jesse said. He spread the sheet of parchment on the floor. Then he took out the tinderbox and began to strike the flint against the ring. The first strike got a spark. The second strike got a bigger spark. The third strike would surely light the wick.

"Give me that," said Emmy. She reached across the table and plucked the tinderbox from Jesse's hands.

"Hey!" he said, lunging for it. But Emmy held it out of his reach.

"This is the property of the Claus. I will return it to him *after* you two have signed the contract."

Jesse shot a look of desperation at Daisy.

Daisy hopped down from the chair. She

marched over to Emmy and stared up at her. "Emmy, we'll be happy to sign the contract."

Jesse stared at Daisy as if she had just sprouted antlers. "We will?"

Daisy smiled serenely. "We think it's wonderful that Santa is going to be your new Keeper," she said, sauntering back to Jesse. "Don't we, Jess?"

"We do?" Jesse said.

Daisy elbowed him hard.

"We do!" he said to Emmy, rubbing his side.

"The Claus will appreciate your compliance," said Emmy.

Daisy paced before the giant fireplace. Unlike the one in their room, this one had no flame in it, cold or otherwise. "When I think that you, Emerald of Leandra, are going to single-handedly change the way Christmas is celebrated, I feel lucky just to witness the new dawning. Sure, Christmas has always been a wonderful time. But now, thanks to you, it will be a *magical* time. It will transform the way children's minds grow and develop! Who knows, maybe it will eventually make world peace more than just a dream."

Jesse stared at his cousin in wonderment.

"And to ensure that this miracle happens," Daisy went on, "we're willing to sign over our

Keepership to Jolly Old St. Nick. Right, Jess?"

"Absolutely!" Jesse said, pounding his fist into his palm.

"We've brought the quill and ink to sign it with, haven't we, Jess?" Daisy said.

Jesse nodded. He rolled up the contract and tucked it under his arm, just in case Emmy decided to swipe it as she had the tinderbox.

"But here's the thing of it, Em," Daisy said. "I won't be able to sign my name with these hands."

Daisy peeled off her mittens and held them up to Emmy. Her hands were pinkish blue and chapped. "Feel?" She went over and placed them on the tender inside of Emmy's hind leg.

Emmy's toe talons shrank away. "Your core temperature is woefully low!" she cried.

"I'll tell you what, Emmy," said Daisy. "If you'll use those mighty jaws of flame to make me a nice cozy fire in the fireplace, I bet my core temperature will warm right up. And *then* I'll be able to sign the contract. Plan?"

"I will do as you say!" said Emmy.

The cousins looked on sadly as Emmy balled up the sheets of stationery and tossed them into the fireplace.

"Stand back," Emmy said.

"Don't we need logs or something?" Jesse said.

"The paper will be sufficient," Emmy said.

Jesse and Daisy huddled behind Emmy's back and peered around. Emmy took a deep breath and blew out. A bright orange flame leapt from her mouth and into the fireplace, striking the ball of paper. It caught fire instantly.

"There you go, Daisy," said Emmy. "Now raise your core temperature. Before the fireplace melts and the Claus gets angry with me."

Daisy and Jesse circled around Emmy and stood with their backs to the fire. Daisy nudged Jesse with her hip. Jesse nodded. He'd kept the scroll behind his back as they moved to the fire. Now he fed the end of the scroll into the flames. He heard a satisfying crackling sound as the scroll began to burn.

Jesse shoved the rest of the scroll into the fire. The fire flared up behind them with a mighty *whump,* sending Jesse and Daisy scooting forward.

Emmy lifted her snout into the air. Her nostrils twitched. "What smells like burning yak?" she asked. Then she looked into the fire and spied the scroll in flames.

"Nooooo!" she cried, scrambling toward the fireplace.

But it was too late. The scroll was engulfed by flame. Not even Emmy could save it now.

"Oh, no!" Emmy howled, opening her mouth wide. Jesse saw his opportunity. He reached into his hoodie pocket, took the last of Miss Alodie's cracker, and tossed it into her big pink maw. Jesse and Daisy watched as the piece of cracker sailed down her throat and disappeared. Emmy swallowed it with a loud gulp.

There was a moment of stillness, like the calm before the storm.

"Look at her eyes, Jess!" said Daisy.

Emmy's eyes had begun to spin like a pair of bright red pinwheels. Red smoke poured out of her nostrils.

"Miss Alodie's cracker is working on her, too," Daisy whispered to Jesse.

When the red smoke thinned, Emmy's eyes stopped spinning and gradually turned green again. Then she threw back her head and let out a heart-rending wail. "Oh, my Keepers!" she cried. "What have I done?" Giant tears slid out of her eyes and rolled down her snout.

Daisy reached into the backpack for her bandana. "What you've done is good," she said soothingly, reaching up to catch the tears. It was a vain effort. There were too many of them, and dragon tears are hot. Where the drops hit the floor, they sizzled and left golf ball–sized dents.

Daisy continued, "You've eaten the cracker and broken the spell."

Behind them, the fire was quickly going out as it consumed the last of Emmy's stationery. The heat of the fire had melted the fireplace into a sludgy mound of ice.

"I feel *terrible!*" Emmy wept. "I've done a no-good, awful, terrible, very bad thing."

"But everything's fine now," Jesse said. "You're back to your old self."

"The spell might be broken," said Emmy, taking the bandana from Daisy and blowing her nose with a loud honk. "But the damage is done!"

"What damage is that?" Daisy asked, stuffing the sodden bandana into the side pouch of the backpack.

"Santa Claus asked me to give him a special present this Christmas," Emmy said.

"We know, Em," Jesse said. "But the thing is, he's not Santa."

"I see that now," said Emmy. "I see now that he is the notorious dragon slayer Beowulf. But when I thought he was Santa Claus, he asked me for a Christmas present, something only I could give him. And who could deny Santa a Christmas present?"

"Absolutely no one," Daisy said gently. "In your

shoes, I'd have done the same thing."

"I don't have shoes," Emmy said. "But *anyway,* Santa asked me for a brace of Thunder Eggs."

"Oh, no," Jesse said. Thunder Eggs were geodes containing baby dragons. For a dragon slayer to get his hands on a supply of baby dragons would be good for the dragon slayer but very bad for the babies.

"You see, that's what the Toyland Vortex machine does," Emmy said. "It isn't really for making toys—although he spelled me into thinking it was. It's really a Vortex Interceptor."

Jesse and Daisy gave her a wary look. "What's that?" they asked.

Emmy heaved a sigh. "It's a machine that's designed to intercept dragon eggs as they enter the earth's atmosphere from the Time Before."

"How exactly does that work?" Jesse asked.

"Well," Emmy began, "you know that dragon eggs, otherwise known as Thunder Eggs, rain down from the heavens."

Daisy nodded. "Just like it says in Native American lore," she said.

Emmy went on. "They come from the Time Before, hurtling through space and time. What no one but dragons—and it seems Beowulf, and now you—know is that the eggs penetrate the earth's atmosphere at the North Pole. From there a swirling vortex sucks them down through the earth's crust to the core. From the molten center of the earth, the Thunder Eggs are then distributed to all the Realms for which their natures destine them: Airy, Watery, Fiery, Earthly."

"Nifty," said Jesse.

"I, daughter of Leandra, who was, in turn, daughter of Tourmaline, am a second-generation earthborn dragon. *Autochthonous* is another word for what I am. Autochthonous dragons are very rare, my mother tells me. Most dragons are Ethereal, which means they are hatched from Thunder Eggs that arrive from the Time Before. What I did under Beowulf's spell was intercept a bunch of Ethereals on their way to earth."

"Not so nifty," said Daisy.

"I told him I couldn't do it while he was breathing down my neck. I waited until he was out, searching for his lost reindeer. When he came back, he knew I had succeeded. He asked me for the eggs. But something in me wouldn't give up those eggs. Even though I was still under his power, it was like this little voice deep inside me said, 'Emmy, do not give the eggs to this man!' So I didn't. I hid them and pretended I was saving them for a surprise."

"So even deep under his spell, there was a part of you that resisted Beowulf's power," said Daisy.

"A really strong part of yourself," Jesse added. "Emmy, we're proud of you."

"That's why he wants to be my Keeper," said Emmy sorrowfully. "If he is my Keeper, I can deny him nothing, including the Thunder Eggs. He can also get me to work the machine and bring in *more* Thunder Eggs whenever he wants."

"Don't worry," said Daisy. "We won't let him be your Keeper, will we, Jess?"

"*We're* your Keepers, Em. And always will be," said Jesse. "There's just one thing I don't understand. I can understand how easily Daisy and I fell under Beowulf's masking spell, but how did he get to you?"

Emmy thought for a moment. "I think," she said, "that Beowulf might have been the Fang Fairy."

"*What?*" Jesse and Daisy chimed.

"Remember the fang I lost? I'm betting Beowulf stole it and used it to work a powerful spell on me. Of course, it helped that I wanted to believe in Santa with all my heart."

"I guess it figures," Daisy said. "Fake Santa. Fake Fang Fairy."

"The next thing you know," Jesse said, "he'll be

putting on a pair of long fuzzy ears and pretending to be the Easter Bunny."

"I think he'd rather be my Keeper," said Emmy.

"So where did you hide the eggs?" Daisy asked.

Emmy held her paws palms up. "In the snow!"

Jesse rolled his eyes. "This is the North Pole, Emmy. There's nothing *but* snow."

"In a mound, in the snow, I don't know, I can't remember where! I was under a spell and my brain was all furry."

"Fuzzy," Jesse said.

"Oh, I am a very bad dragon," she howled. "I *deserve* to have Beowulf as my Keeper."

"Don't say that, Emmy!" said Daisy. "You need to have a positive attitude, and we need to have a plan."

But before they had concocted so much as a glimmer of a plan, there came a deafening pounding on the door.

"It's him!" Emmy whispered frantically. "Quick! Hide!"

Emmy picked them up and put them on her ice bed, covered them with a fur quilt, then tossed the tinderbox and the backpack in after them. With one finger, Jesse held up a corner of the quilt so they could see out. Just before the door opened, the room lit up with a sudden green flare of light.

The man who stormed into Emmy's room no longer bore the slightest resemblance to Santa Claus. He didn't even look much like the man in the photographs in the man cave. Or rather, he was a supercharged version of that man. Instead of a suit, he was wearing a stiff leather skirt and a leather vest. His arms and thighs were bare, scarred, and bulging with muscle. He wore scuffed leather gauntlets on his hands and high leather boots on his feet. Beneath an ox-horned helmet, his beard was white and his hair was plaited into two thick braids.

While he might have been wearing a woman's hairstyle, there was nothing womanish about him. The strong bones of his face looked chiseled from stone. From beneath bushy white eyebrows, his pale blue eyes burned with a fierce, predatory light. This, as anyone with sense could see, was a warrior. And the heavy broadsword hanging from his studded belt confirmed it.

"Where is my Christmas present?" he said to Emmy. "I have waited long enough."

"You're not Santa Claus," Emmy said, leaning against the sagging mantelpiece. "What's more, you've been a bad, bad boy, and you don't deserve a present from me or anyone else."

Beowulf regarded Emmy through narrowed

eyes. "I see my spell needs some touching up."

"You can't help it if your powers are puny," Emmy said, smiling and showing all her fangs.

Daisy fumbled for Jesse's hand and squeezed it hard. Jesse's heart was hammering so loudly he was afraid the big man would hear it.

Beowulf walked over to what was left of the fireplace and poked the ashes with the toe of his boot.

"They were here," he grunted. "Where are your Keepers? I'll draw up another contract, and this one, they will sign under duress."

Emmy blew on her talons and polished them on her chest. "There's a fat chance of that," she said. "And oh, by the way, I love your dress."

"WHERE ARE THEY?" he thundered.

"You just missed them," Emmy said, yawning widely.

Beowulf stalked around the room, flinging open doors and peering beneath the table and the chairs. Finally, he came over to the bed. Jesse could hear the angry breath whistling in and out of his nose. They were lying as flat as they could, but would he see suspicious lumps under the quilt?

Jesse squeezed his eyes shut.

Beowulf whipped the quilt off the bed. Jesse felt the frigid air hitting his back. When nothing happened, Jesse dared to open one eye.

Beowulf was leaning down, staring right at him with eyes of searing icy blue. He was so close that Jesse could see the red veins on his nose and smell the red meat and mead on his breath. Jesse opened his mouth to yelp, but Daisy clamped her hand over his face.

Beowulf straightened and continued to search the room. Daisy looked at Jesse and mouthed the words "invisibility spell."

Suddenly, Jesse understood. The green flash just before the door had opened—Emmy had cast an invisibility spell over them.

The cousins lay there not daring to move a muscle lest Beowulf sense a stirring in the air even if he couldn't see them. After he completed his search, Beowulf returned to Emmy and unsheathed his sword. It had a gem-studded hilt and a long blade with a jagged line running diagonally across it where it had been mended.

"Come with me, she-dragon!" Beowulf said.

Emmy drew herself up on her hind legs. Just as she took the deep breath that came before she summoned a spell, Beowulf touched the tip of his sword to Emmy's chin.

Instantly, Emmy deflated like a blow-up dragon

with a steady leak. She dropped down off her hind legs and hunched onto her elbows. The light in her eyes dimmed and her scales faded from green to gray.

The cousins were all too familiar with what they were seeing, sadly. It was iron poisoning. Dragons are strong and magical beings, but iron makes them as weak and powerless as lambs.

Jesse thought he saw a stuttering green light rise up around the bed. He suspected that Emmy's invisibility spell had weakened. If Beowulf were to turn around, he would see the two of them huddled on the ice bed. Jesse held his breath, but Beowulf marched Emmy out the door and slammed it behind them.

Jesse pressed his hot, sweaty cheek to the cold, hard surface of the ice bed. "That was close," he said. "I think that was Naegling."

"What?" Daisy asked, sitting up. "Now I'm really confused. I thought that was Beowulf."

"It was. Naegling is the name of his sword," Jesse said. "Beowulf had a few swords. The sword called Hrunting was engraved. Naegling had gems studding its hilt, and he broke it once. I guess its blade is iron, which is why Emmy weakened."

"And he'll use it to finish her off if we don't

figure out a way to rescue her," said Daisy.

"He won't kill her," Jesse said. "He wouldn't get his dragon eggs without her."

Daisy hugged herself and shivered. "And what are we supposed to do? He's a big, scary brute in a leather skirt with a sword."

Jesse clucked his tongue. "If the professor could hear you now, do you know what he'd say? He'd say, 'Stop blubbing!'"

Daisy squared her shoulders. "He'd say, 'You are Dragon Keepers. Figure it out.'"

"Exactly," said Jesse. "Let's start by getting our snowshoes back."

"Really?" Daisy asked in surprise.

"I don't know about you," said Jesse, "but when Beowulf came through that door, I sweated my thermal pads into warm Jell-O."

Daisy nodded and shivered. "Me too."

"Remember how when we first arrived at the North Pole, the snowshoes kept us warm?" Jesse asked.

Daisy nodded. "Until he made us take them off. Then we were freezing until we put on his snowsuits."

"Without Miss Alodie's blue goo cracker, those snowshoes are the only magical advantage we have,"

Jesse said. "And I figure we need all the help we can get."

"Let's go get them, then," Daisy said. She grabbed the backpack and slid off the bed.

Jesse tucked the tinderbox into the side pouch. They opened the door and headed back toward the main entrance, passing a sculpture of a troll where there had once been Frosty, and a wolf where there had once been Rudolph.

When they got to the entrance hall, they found their snowshoes exactly where they had left them. The statue of Santa and the child that had been in the center of the room was now a statue of Beowulf and a troll.

Daisy fell upon the snowshoes and fastened them on. "Oh, Jess," she said, a blissful expression spreading across her face. "I'm warm again."

Jesse bent over to put on his snowshoes. Daisy was right. No sooner were the snowshoes back on his feet than he felt the blood rushing back into his fingers and toes. "Okay! Let's go get our dragon back," Jesse said.

They were just climbing to their feet when a band of trolls appeared at the other end of the hall. The trolls were armed with ice axes. When they saw Jesse and Daisy, they came pounding toward

them, brandishing the axes and yodeling and gurgling with a sound like bubbling oil. Oddly, they
still wore Santa's-helper hats on their hideous
lumpy heads, so as they bore down upon Jesse and
Daisy, the sound of their claws scratching the ice
was accompanied by the cheery jingle of holiday
bells.

There was only one way for Jesse and Daisy to
go. Together, they pushed open the front door and
fled into the never-ending arctic night.

CHAPTER SEVEN

THE AURORA

Jesse and Daisy flew across the arctic crust as if Miss Alodie's snowshoes had sprouted wings. Daisy caught a brief glimpse of their pursuers over her shoulder. With their long fangs and their bulbous eyes, their humped backs and their gangling limbs, they looked like giant, hairy spiders.

The snowy terrain was full of surprises. There were rolling hills and icy ramps leading to sharp drop-offs, which they leapt, flying through the air and landing flat on their snowshoes at the bottom. Now and then, there were breaks in the snow where they had to leap over pools of freezing water and land on the other side without breaking stride.

At first the trolls moved slowly, dragging their ice axes behind them. Then they wised up and shoved the ice axes into their shoulder straps. After that, they barreled along on their hairy knuckles, their claws digging into the snow and lending them speed and traction. The gap between them and Jesse and Daisy narrowed.

Before long Daisy could smell them, a mixture of decaying fish and steaming tar. "Wait a minute," she said, gasping for breath. "Stop."

"Stop?" Jesse gasped in return. "They'll be all over us!"

"In that book from Miss Alodie's store? It said trolls fear live flame."

Jesse slid to a halt. He reached into the backpack's side pouch and took out the tinderbox. "Get me something to make a torch."

Jesse knelt over the tinderbox while Daisy tore into the side pouch of the backpack. "What about this?" She held up the bandana soaked with dragon tears and boogers.

"That could work," Jesse said.

Daisy dug out the flashlight and tied one corner of the bandana around it, making a kind of torch.

Jesse struck the flint against the ring, and a spark leapt up.

"I hope it will burn. It's still kind of soggy," Daisy said.

With the next spark, the bandana burst into flames. Daisy held the makeshift torch at arm's length.

"Wow!" Jesse said, little orange flames dancing in his eyes. "It really worked!"

"It's about time you summoned us," a familiar voice called out.

"Who said that?" Jesse asked, looking around.

"I think it's coming from the torch," Daisy said. "Look!"

Out of the torch's fire poked a pointy orange head made of flame.

Daisy grinned. "It's Spark!"

"Hey, you guys!" another voice said. This voice belonged to a small flame that flickered white one moment, blue the next. It was the Fire Fairy named Flicker.

Then a third voice called out, "Let's show these

trolls how we do things in the Fiery Realm!" Jesse and Daisy saw a little red ball of flame next to the other Fire Fairies. It was their friend Fiero.

"You guys scram," Fiero continued. "We'll take it from here."

Daisy and Jesse had made friends with the Fire Fairies when they'd followed Emmy down a volcano's crater into the Fiery Realm, where they prevented St. George and Sadra from mining the gems in the Great Grotto. Ever since, the fairies occasionally popped up in a fire to say hello. This visit was most fortuitous.

"You sure you'll be okay?" Jesse asked.

"Are you kidding?" Fiero said. "Dragon snot makes great fuel. We might just burn forever."

"You kids run along and do what needs doing," Spark told them.

Daisy shrugged, then put the torch down on the snow. She and Jesse took a step backward.

Tha-whump! A wall of flame shot up. Jesse and Daisy watched as, the very next moment, the band of trolls came vaulting over the rise.

When the trolls saw the fire, they flipped onto their backs and covered their faces with their long, hairy arms, like vampires shrinking before sunlight. They burst into a jibber-jabber of pain and outrage.

"Back to the palace for Emmy!" Daisy shouted.

Giving both the fire and the trolls a wide berth, Jesse and Daisy circled back the way they had come. But every time they crested a hill, instead of seeing the palace's spires, all they saw were darkness and ice and snow.

"We're lost," Daisy said, coming to a hopeless standstill.

Jesse stopped a few feet away from her and nodded grimly. "Pretty much."

"Doesn't Blueberry Sal have a navigation tool?" Daisy asked.

"Yeah," said Jesse, "but I seriously doubt that Beowulf's palace is registered on GPS maps."

"Try it anyway, and see what you get," said Daisy.

Jesse reached around behind Daisy to get the Blueberry out of the backpack, then pulled off his mittens with his teeth and started thumbing the keyboard. The tiny glowing screen cast a pale blue light across his face.

"Anything?" Daisy asked.

Jesse mumbled something around the mittens that sounded like "Gimme a sec."

Meanwhile, Daisy scanned the starry heavens for some sign of the aurora borealis, but it was nowhere to be found. She thought back to the fire in their palace sitting room. Had the cold green and red flame been the Aurora trying to contact her? Had she, like Emmy back on the barn roof, been unable to understand it? And having been ignored by both Emmy and Daisy, had the aurora given up?

Jesse took the mittens out of his mouth and pointed to his left. "Blueberry Sal says that the exact North Pole is about a quarter of a mile in that direction."

"Remember the diagram of the Vortex Interceptor in Beowulf's man cave?" Daisy said. "It was sitting right on top of the North Pole, wasn't it?"

Jesse nodded. "Maybe Beowulf took Emmy there."

They set out, and after a while, they didn't need Blueberry Sal to guide them. Lights appeared up ahead—neither the cold blue magical lights of the palace nor the colorful lights of the aurora borealis. Soon they came to a ring of floodlights illuminating a structure that looked just like the diagram in the man cave, like a cross between an oil derrick and the Eiffel Tower—only much, much taller.

"I wonder how high it is," Daisy said.

Jesse's eyes took on a hard gleam. "I don't care how high it is. Beowulf created it to intercept and collect Thunder Eggs. As Dragon Keepers, we have only one choice." He turned to Daisy. "We have to destroy it."

"But how, Jess? It's made of metal girders," Daisy said. "We're not strong enough to pull them down."

Jesse glanced around and noticed a pile of tools lying in the snow nearby. He went over and picked up a wrench. "If we can find the machine's motor and toss this monkey wrench into it, that should take it permanently off-line," Jesse said.

"Is that really a monkey wrench?" Daisy asked.

"I have no idea, but it will have to do," Jesse said solemnly.

Daisy scanned the ground underneath the structure. She saw scrap metal and tools, but nothing that looked like an engine. "I don't see the motor, do you?" she asked Jesse.

"If it's not at the bottom," he said, "then it must be . . ."

They craned their heads as they looked up the side of the tower. The tower was so high, they couldn't see its top.

There was only one thing to do. Daisy handed the backpack to Jesse and took off her snowshoes. She felt the cold the instant they were off her feet. She held her hand out for the monkey wrench, and Jesse slapped it into her palm. She shoved it into the back pocket of her jeans.

She stood back and examined the structure

again. It was made of countless diamond-shaped struts. Moving to one of the tower's legs, she grabbed on to the struts with her mittened hands, then fit her left foot in the bottom of one diamond and her right foot in the bottom of a higher one. She started climbing.

"Be careful!" Jesse said.

Daisy nodded. Except for the girders biting into the soles of her fuzzy white boots, the climbing was easy. With the wind whistling in her ears, she climbed higher and higher. She had never climbed anything this high. After a while, she stopped to rest and looked down.

On the other side of the tower, huge fissures stretched across the ice. She called down to Jesse and described them.

"Maybe the Interceptor causes them," Jesse shouted up. "Or maybe that's just the polar ice, breaking up and reforming. Are you there yet?"

"Not yet." Daisy kept climbing.

The next time she stopped and looked down, Jesse looked no bigger than a chipmunk in a plaid coat. Daisy let go long enough to wave. Then she looked up and continued to climb.

She climbed until her hands in their mittens were so cold she could no longer feel them. It was as if she had borrowed someone else's hands.

Someone else's hands gripped the icy girders. She hoped that someone else was really strong. It was a long way down.

Finally, she came to within six diamonds of the pointed top of the tower. The topmost girders looked as if a substance like colorful paraffin had melted all over them. On the tip-top, sparks leapt and crackled.

Daisy might not have been afraid of heights, but she was petrified of electricity. This was as far as she dared to go. And still there was no motor to be seen. The mechanism obviously ran on magic. And you couldn't throw a monkey wrench into magic. Not unless you were a sorcerer.

Disappointed that she wouldn't be able to shut down the machine, she was getting ready to climb back down when she noticed the lights of the palace off to the right. Now she and Jesse would know which direction to go to get back. But then she noticed something else, too. It was in the snow between the tower and the palace. She squinted. Either her eyes were playing tricks on her, or it was a mound of snow with a big smiley face on it with two fangs.

As always happens, the climb down seemed vastly shorter than the climb up. She was also moving at top speed, in a hurry to get to Jesse and tell him what she'd seen from the top of the tower.

"Jesse!" Daisy said breathlessly as she reached the ground. "There was no motor, but I think I found Emmy's hiding place for the Thunder Eggs she intercepted!"

Jesse didn't answer her and he didn't move. At first Daisy was concerned that he might have frozen stiff while she was gone. But his eyes were bright and alert and wary.

"Jesse!" she said. "Did you hear me?"

"Shhhhh," he said, gesturing with his chin.

Daisy turned to see what he was looking at.

Just beyond the perimeter of the floodlights, a pair of eyes glowed red in the darkness.

Daisy caught her breath. "Is that a troll?" she asked.

Jesse shook his head minutely. "It's a wolf," he whispered. "It's been standing there staring at me for the longest time. So far, it hasn't moved."

Then, as if it heard what Jesse said, the beast paced forward into the light. Like the ice sculptures outside Beowulf's man cave come to life, it was huge and white. Its coat was long and shaggy. And it was wearing a brightly colored embroidered harness.

"I think that might be Blitzen," Jesse whispered. "Santa's missing reindeer."

In slow motion, Daisy bent down and slipped on her snowshoes. If St. Nick was really Beowulf and the elves were really trolls, then it made a kind of crazy sense that the reindeer would be wolves.

As soon as Daisy had tightened the last tie on her snowshoes, she straightened and nodded in the direction she'd seen lights. "The palace is that way," she said quietly.

Jesse nodded back. "Then let's . . . run!" he shouted. "Back to the palace!"

The two of them dashed away. Behind them came the steady *thud-thud-thud* of the beast's feet hitting the snow at a dead run.

We'll never make it, Daisy thought desperately. *We can't outrun a wolf.* She turned and flung the wrench at the pursuing creature but missed and still the wolf came at them. It was like one of those bad dreams where you're running as fast as you can but it still feels like you're swimming through molasses.

As they crested the next hill, the towers of the palace shone blue against the night sky.

"There it is!" Daisy panted.

They headed down into another gully. Behind them, the wolf snarled. Daisy could feel the heat of its breath as its jaws snapped at her heels. They ran up the side of the gulley, expecting to see the turrets of the palace piercing the sky like icicles.

Suddenly, the ground fell out from beneath them, sending them flying through the air. They found themselves sliding down an icy incline, with the wolf tumbling after them. By the time they saw where they were headed, it was too late to stop.

Just ahead, the bottom of the icy slope dropped off into thin air. They had overshot the palace and gone straight to the edge of the abyss.

Daisy reached out for Jesse's hand. If they were going to tumble into the abyss, they were going to do it together.

Suddenly, right where the ice ended and the nothingness began, a bridge of bright red and green lights appeared in the air. Jesse and Daisy slid directly from the ice onto the light bridge. To their astonishment, the bridge held their weight.

Gingerly, they stood up and tested the light bridge by stamping their feet. It seemed as solid as if it had been made of long strips of red and green stone.

Unfortunately, the bridge also held the wolf's weight. Jesse and Daisy sprinted along the bridge as the wolf slowly got to its feet, confused. Jesse glanced over his shoulder as they fled, then scooted to a stop.

"Look!" he cried, pointing behind them.

Daisy looked back and saw that as the wolf began to stalk slowly toward them, the lights of the bridge began to fade. With a sudden yelp, the wolf plummeted, head over tail, into the abyss.

That's when they heard it, a sound like melting icicles, each drop a distinct musical note. It started out as a faint and delicate plinking sound, then swelled in volume as the red and green lights they were standing on rose up and surrounded them with all the colors of the spectrum and a bright, throbbing music.

There were voices in the music, a chorus of sparkling chimes ringing in the icy air. Daisy thought of the lights in the sky behind the barn back home, the lights in their palace room's fireplace, the lights in the polar sky. They were all, she thought, one and the same. They were the aurora borealis, and they had been calling to them, first to Emmy and now to her and Jesse. Perhaps because she was no longer just looking at the light but submerged in it, she understood it at last.

"Do you hear them, Jess?" she cried out over the music. Jesse nodded.

The voices sang:

We are the Aurora!
Behold and take heed.

A monarch of yore
Has done a dire deed.

The drill he hath built
to bore into the sky
harms the Aurora.
In great numbers, we die!

The Aurora will perish,
And after we go,
The earth will soon follow.
This much we know.

The singing stopped. Jesse and Daisy stared at each other, eyes wide.

"Monarch of yore," Jesse said. "That must be Beowulf."

"This explains why the Aurora was trying to contact Emmy back in Goldmine City," Daisy said. "The Vortex Interceptor is hurting them."

"Not only that, they seem to think it's endangering the whole earth. I bet it has something to do with the ozone layer. The ozone layer protects the earth from the harmful rays of the sun. If the Interceptor is destroying the ozone, we have to do something fast." Jesse looked into the lights and said, "What can we do?"

The Aurora didn't respond. Jesse tried another tack. He didn't have much of a singing voice and he couldn't rhyme his way out of a paper bag, but maybe it was the only way to get through to them. He sang:

> We aren't the type
> Who ever would shirk.
> But Beowulf's powerful.
> What tactics will work?

Daisy gave him a look, but he shrugged. It was the best he could do off the top of his head. And it seemed to work, because the next moment, the Aurora sang:

> We need the dragon
> We have summoned forth.
> Only she can defeat
> The foe from the north.

It was Daisy who piped up this time:

> Emerald's been captured
> By this evil Dane.
> His big iron sword
> Made her powers wane.

Jesse cleared his throat and said, "Um, Daise? I think we've pretty much established that the dude's Norwegian, not Danish."

Daisy said, "Lots of luck finding something to rhyme with *that*." Then she sang on:

> We are her Keepers
> and he wants us to sign
> her over to him
> on the dotted line.

This time, Jesse gave her a big thumbs-up. The lights sang back:

> Here in the North
> We are happy to say
> there are tricks of the light
> The Aurora can play.

> In this frozen wasteland
> Of perpetual night
> We urge you to join
> The Army of Light.

Jesse and Daisy gave each other a look, then turned to the Aurora and said, "We're in!"

CHAPTER EIGHT

A TRICK OF THE LIGHT

The moment Beowulf took out the iron sword, Emmy said to herself, *Emerald, old girl, it serves you right!*

Considering that she had not only been taken in by Beowulf's Santa Claus masking spell, but had actually gone to work for him, she deserved to have her powers stripped. She dragged herself along after Beowulf as he went to his study and hunched over his desk, quill scratching across parchment, drawing up a new contract. When he was finished, he rolled it up and stuck it in his belt.

Afterward, he stalked around the ice palace, rounding up trolls. It was a big palace, and it seemed to take a very long time. And all the while, he grew increasingly frustrated, as if there were fewer trolls than he expected to find. Emmy wondered whether the trolls, like Blitzen, had run off somewhere. When Beowulf had gathered as many trolls as he could muster, he led them outside.

Oh, how Emmy wished they had stayed inside! Sure, it was as cold as a freezer compartment in there, but at least there was no wind. With Beowulf's iron sword cutting into her powers, she was keenly sensitive to the cold. The arctic winds slid beneath her scales like a thousand ice picks.

As if all this weren't bad enough, a band of trolls armed with ice axes shambled along behind her like a parade of trained apes. Despite her waning powers, her nose worked all too well. There was only one word for the way trolls smelled: *malanky*.

When they arrived at the Vortex Interceptor, Beowulf frowned. He walked around and around the base of the machine. "They have been here," he muttered. "Those two children have been here, and they have been meddling."

"Your precious machine is still standing," Emmy said. "What's the problem?"

She too saw her Keepers' snowshoe tracks, but she also saw the tracks of a big wolf. She began to fret.

Beowulf swung around to Emmy. "Did you tell them where to find the Thunder Eggs?"

"Why would I do that?" Emmy snapped. "They'd never be able to protect them from you."

Beowulf nodded thoughtfully. "I believe you. But now you will tell me where you have hidden the eggs."

"You're the Easter Bunny," Emmy said. "Find them yourself."

"Bah! You are a maddening creature." He shouted to the trolls, "Go and search for the eggs! They can't be far from here! They will be buried in the snow."

The trolls, grumbling, stomped off in all directions. Emmy heard the steady *chunk-chunk-chunk* of their ice axes hitting the snow.

"I will search, too," he said. He took up a shovel from among the tools lying in the snow at the base of the Interceptor. "You," he said to Emmy, stabbing the sword into the snow next to her. "Stay here and don't move."

Emmy couldn't have moved if she had tried. The power of the iron sword nearly paralyzed her. She had been in fixes before: trussed in chains by St. George in Queen Hap's hobgoblin throne room, and stuck in the deep-sea diver's helmet in which Maldew the Mermage had confined her. But there was something about this particular fix that made all the other fixes seem like a walk in the dark.

Or was it a walk in the *park*?

She had no idea which was right. It was certainly dark enough at the North Pole, so maybe this really was a walk in the dark, in which case, those other fixes were walks in the light?

Without Jesse's guidance, she was lost. She missed Daisy every bit as much. Daisy was so brave. Just being around Daisy made Emmy's courage soar.

"Where are you, my Keepers?" she wondered aloud. "Are you safe from the wolf?"

Beowulf, who was about thirty paces away, heard her. He stopped digging and leaned on his shovel. "Wherever they are, I hope they return soon."

Emmy snapped, "I hope they are a million, trillion miles away from here, because I no longer deserve to have them as Keepers."

"Now you're making sense," said Beowulf with a wolfish grin. "You deserve me. Your Keepers are bound to come here, sooner or later, to rescue you. And when they do, I will threaten to harm you, and they will sign the contract. It will be that simple. After they sign, I will put you to work intercepting eggs for me, your perfect Keeper."

Emmy stared up at the scaffold and thought back to before the adventure started, when she'd been sitting on her barn roof, watching the colored lights in the sky. Now she knew that the singing she'd heard had been an SOS from the Aurora, the spirits of the northern lights. She'd been on the brink of understanding their song when Beowulf had come along in his sleigh, masked as Santa.

Now she saw with her own eyes what Beowulf's spell had prevented her from seeing before, that the machine Beowulf had designed to intercept Thunder Eggs also pierced the ozone layer, the same area of the sky where the Aurora dwelled. The sharp top, which crackled with elemental power, was all hung about with the limp husks of dead light spirits.

Not only had Emmy not helped the Aurora, but she had thrown her lot in with their enemy.

Beowulf probably didn't even know he was hurting the Aurora. He didn't care who he hurt. All he cared about was getting his hands on Thunder Eggs. Beowulf was a bad man, worse than St. George on his worst day. Maybe it was a good thing that she couldn't remember where she had hidden the eggs. Maybe the eggs were better off lost forever in a frozen wasteland than in the clutches of a man who wanted to hatch them only to drink their blood and extend his life.

Emmy had to wonder what her mother would say if she knew what Emmy had done. There was a better word for Emmy than *autochthonous*. It was *traitor*! Oh, if only she could regain her powers and redeem herself.

Emmy was just about to open her mouth and tell Beowulf that Jesse and Daisy would never sign her over to him when her tongue stuck to the roof of her mouth. It was frozen stiff. The arctic temperatures were freezing Emmy, encasing her in an ever-thickening coat of ice. Inch by inch, scale by scale, with a creaking sound like a giant door shutting, the ice was stealing over her body.

Beowulf stopped his digging and approached her, his arms folded across his muscled chest. "I prefer you like this," he said with a laugh. "It will keep you out of trouble until you are completely mine. You should be pleased. With the continual supply of dragon blood you will provide me, your Keeper will be not only the king of Geatland but also the king of the world. Because the man who lives forever rules forever."

Just then, Jesse and Daisy came sliding on their snowshoes toward the Interceptor. Emmy no longer had the power to cry out, as she wanted to with every fiber of her being. Oh, how she wanted to scream at her Keepers to run away before it was too late!

Frantically, Emmy tried to send them Mind Messages, but her Mind Message Center was out of order.

"I thought you'd return," Beowulf growled at them.

Jesse and Daisy stopped just outside the ring of floodlights. The trolls dropped their shovels and moved closer, looking on with their goggle eyes. Beowulf started toward them as well, but Jesse raised his arm. "Keep your distance, Buster," he said.

"Yeah, we don't want to catch any dragon slayer cooties," Daisy said. "And don't even think of siccing the trolls on us."

Inwardly, Emmy beamed with pride. How brave they were, her Keepers! How noble and forthright! And how *sassy*!

Jesse said, "We've changed our minds about signing our dragon over to you. If you want to draw up another contract, we'll sign it."

For a moment, Emmy was shocked. *Her* Keepers would never willingly give up their title! It wasn't an easy job being a Dragon Keeper, but they liked it and were good at it.

Then Emmy thought about all the grief she had brought to them over the months they had been together. Still, surely the good times outweighed the bad. It had to be a trick.

Beowulf, apparently thinking the same thing, narrowed his eyes. "Why are you so eager to let her go?"

"Ha!" said Jesse. "Wouldn't *you* like to know?"

"Wait a minute, Jess," said Daisy. "He's entitled to know." Daisy turned to Beowulf. "It's a lot of work being a Dragon Keeper."

"Yeah, we never get to play like regular kids anymore," Jesse said. "We want to go back to the way things were before we found that Thunder Egg, back to being mindless and irresponsible. But we can't just give our dragon up for adoption. There are no adoption agencies for dragons. So you see, you've solved the problem for us."

Inwardly, Emmy sagged. It wasn't a trick after all. Her Keepers really *did* want to give her up. If that was the case, then all was lost and she no longer cared what happened to her or to any dragons, Autochthonous or Ethereal.

"Oh, and by the way, where *is* our dragon?" said Jesse.

"She's standing right in front of you," said Beowulf. "Like a mastodon, perfectly preserved in ice."

Jesse flicked his eyes over at Emmy. And that was when Emmy saw it. There was something not quite right about Jesse's eyes. Emmy had been so busy listening to what her Keepers were saying that she had failed to notice how they looked. But now she saw that they both looked a bit too shiny and colorful, like pictures in a slick magazine.

Were they under some sort of a spell? Was that why they were so ready to give her up? In that case, spells could be reversed. Hope stirred in Emmy's breast. Perhaps all was not lost.

"But we do have one condition," said Daisy. "First, you have to throw that iron sword into the abyss."

"Once you've done that," said Jesse, "you can

go back to the palace and draw up another contract."

"We'll sign it," said Daisy. "And she'll be all yours."

Beowulf seemed to be thinking it over. At length, he nodded and said, "So be it!"

To Emmy's astonishment, he yanked the sword out of the ice, swung it around and around over his head, and sent it whistling through the air in the direction of the abyss. Immediately, Emmy felt an itching in her talons and in the tip of her snout that meant her magical powers were returning, one teeny-tiny fraction of an inch of her body at a time.

Why had Beowulf thrown away his sword? He had to know that once the sword was gone, her powers would come back.

Then she understood. Her Keepers were thinking that it would take time for Beowulf to return to the palace and redraft the contract, time enough for Emmy's powers to return, and they would be off. They couldn't know that Beowulf had already drawn up the contract and was carrying it with him at this very moment. He would leave her Keepers no choice but to sign the contract—before Emmy's powers had time to return!

"Very well, then," said Beowulf, turning to the Keepers. "I have done what you asked. And as good luck and careful planning would have it, I have already drawn up a new contract."

He pulled the roll of paper out of his belt and unfurled it with a wicked grin.

Oh, if only she could thaw a little more quickly! Emmy had to stop her Keepers from signing, but her powers were maddeningly slow in coming back to her.

Jesse produced Beowulf's ink bottle, and Daisy pulled out his quill and dipped it in the ink.

"Okay, Beowulf," she said, holding out her hand. "Give us the contract. We're ready when you are."

Beowulf stepped past the lights to hand the contract to Daisy, but the contract passed right through her arm! It was as if she were no more than a ghostly apparition. And then it became obvious to everyone—the real Daisy wasn't there. Neither was the real Jesse.

They were both nothing more than a trick of the light.

Their images flickered and began to melt, like statues made of colored sugar, leaving Beowulf snarling, crushing the scroll in his fists.

THE BATTLE OF THE NORTH POLE

It had been almost too easy, like working puppets by remote control. All Jesse and Daisy had to do was stand inside the Aurora as they hovered over the abyss, while a hologram of Beowulf shimmered in front of them. Whatever they said to the Beowulf

132

hologram, their holograms down at the North Pole repeated to the real Beowulf.

Not being physically next to Beowulf made the cousins much bolder. For instance, had Daisy actually been standing face to face with the hulking Norseman, she never would have dreamed of accusing him of having dragon slayer cooties. That would have been nuts! But it was like talking to an actor on a television screen who was playing a very scary character. It was easy and safe and even sort of fun.

And better yet, it had worked. Beowulf had fallen for the trick of the light. He had pitched the iron sword away, assuming he could force them to sign the contract before Emmy had her powers back. He couldn't have been more wrong. And now that Emmy was free, the Army of Light was ready to spring into action.

When the Aurora invited Jesse and Daisy to join the Army of Light, neither had been sure what to expect. The last thing they'd anticipated was that they would be an army of only two.

After the Beowulf hologram disappeared, two patches of light separated them from the Aurora. As the lights approached, they took on shapes that looked a bit like horses, except these horses had sharp snouts and legs that tapered to pencil-point hooves. One was red, and the other was green.

The Aurora sang:

> Mount the light mares
> And ride into the fray.
> They will help you survive
> This tumultuous day.

The light mares had flaming manes. The green mare chose Daisy, and the red one ambled toward Jesse. The cousins grabbed the horses' manes and swung up onto their backs.

"This is great," Jesse said. "But we could use some weapons."

No sooner had Jesse said this than two swords, shimmering with red and green light, appeared in their fists.

The Aurora sang:

> Wield these weapons
> And you'll see that they
> Will serve you well
> This valorous day!

"Now *this* is what I call a light saber!" Jesse said.

The cousins, who had learned how to use swords in the Fiery Realm, didn't have time to test their weapons. Emmy needed their help right now. In moments, they were charging back across the light bridge and pounding over the ice toward the North Pole.

They came upon Emmy not far from the Vortex Interceptor, wrestling with Beowulf. When she saw them, she cried, "My Keepers! And you are riding the Aurora!"

Their light mares and swords were bright enough to illuminate the battlefield, revealing wolves and trolls swarming across the snow toward them.

"I've got Beowulf covered," Emmy called to them. "See if you can sort out the rest of these jokers."

"I'll take the wolves," Daisy said to Jesse. "You take the trolls."

"No, I'll take the wolves," said Jesse. "You take the trolls."

Daisy hesitated. "Trolls it is, then. Good luck."

"Back at you," said Jesse.

At least a dozen trolls came rushing at Daisy, gurgling and howling, their ice axes swinging. Daisy's sword clattered against the ice axes, as useless as a butter knife. *I could use a good ice ax myself,* Daisy thought. And just as the thought entered her head, her sword morphed into an ice ax, twice the size of the trolls'. The Aurora had given her a weapon that read her mind!

She hopped off her light mare, then dug her ax into the snow beneath one of the trolls and flipped it into the air like a huge, hairy Tiddlywink.

Daisy went at the trolls, swinging and hacking and blocking, meeting their ice axes blow for blow. The light mare helped by staying at her back and blocking any rear assaults. But it didn't take Daisy long to discover that the trolls' greatest asset on the battlefield wasn't their ice axes. It was their foul odor. It was so pungent that her eyes smarted. She badly wanted to fight one-handed, with the other hand pinching her nose, but she knew she needed both hands.

Three trolls bore down upon her and backed her into a snowbank. She looked around in panic. She could turn her sword into a snow shovel and dig. Or she could turn it into a staff to hold off all three of them at once. But how long could she hold out?

As she was trying to decide which way to go, one of the trolls ducked under her ax and came at her jabbering. She flattened her hand against its chest and gave it a good hard shove, but in the process her fingers slipped into the damp area under the creature's armpit.

"Gross!" she cried, pulling her hand away and wiping it on the snow. Then she watched as the troll she had just touched burst into giggles and collapsed, rolling on the ground.

Still holding off the other two, Daisy watched the helplessly giggling troll. What was even more amazing than the giggles was that the troll no longer smelled like rotten fish. The giggling troll gave off an aroma like roses. Then, most amazing of all, when the giggling reached its zenith, the troll turned to stone, then crumbled into a big pile of beige dust.

This gave Daisy a brilliant idea. Turning her ice ax into a feather duster, she held off the other two trolls with what Jesse would later call her patented Kitchy-Kitchy-Koo Offense, tickling them under the armpits, under the chin, on their round bellies, anyplace she thought they might be ticklish.

Like the first troll, they were seized by fits of hilarity, filling the air with the smell of roses as they giggled their way to oblivion. After that, Daisy set to work on the rest of the trolls, determined not to stop until she had turned every one of them to dust.

Meanwhile, Jesse galloped toward the wolves,

who were charging at him as if he were a piece of fresh meat.

Jesse had read that wolves were basically afraid of people. He had seen what Daisy had done with her sword, so he turned his sword into a sickle-bladed scimitar, slashing the air and booming forth in his most manly tones, "You boys will git outta Dodge if you know what's good for you!"

This didn't make much of an impression on the wolves. One of them crept beneath the scimitar blade and snapped its jaws.

Jesse backed up his light mare quickly. "Nice wolfie," he said, trying to keep the fear out of his voice. Because he knew that wolves could smell fear, he tried his best to smell brave as the mare dodged the attacking wolves on its nimble feet.

Just then, the Aurora sang in his ear.

> We will offer the wolves
> A tempting treat
> With a trick of the light
> That looks like meat.
>
> Meanwhile, you must
> Evade this strife.
> Heel your mare hard
> And run for your life!

Jesse didn't think twice. He kicked the sides of his light mare and took off, sparing one backward look. The Aurora threw light on the snow that formed mirages of big, juicy cuts of meat to tempt the wolves. The wolves nosed around just long enough to discover the trick, then took off after Jesse.

Jesse's lead melted away too quickly. In moments, the wolves' jaws were snapping at his boot heels. In answer, the light mare leapt into the air and flew above the wolves' heads. The maddened wolves rose up on their hind legs and snarled and snapped at the light mare's pencil-point hooves just out of reach.

Then Jesse remembered what Daisy had said after she had climbed partway up the Vortex Interceptor. She'd seen fissures in the ice not far from the North Pole, even though he hadn't been able to see them from where he had been standing at the time.

Jesse wheeled the light mare around and galloped toward the Interceptor. The wolves, skidding on the snow, followed.

"Up, horsie!" Jesse said to the light mare, tugging on its mane. The light mare rose even higher into the air, allowing Jesse to survey the course ahead of them. Sure enough, on the other side of the Interceptor a deep crack opened up in the ice and snow. It was about as long as a football field and as narrow as an alley.

"Down, horsie!" Jesse said. The mare soared downward as they passed the Interceptor. Her delicate hooves alit once more on the snow just before they leapt headlong into the fissure.

With a series of yelps and howls, the wolves piled in after them. When the last one had charged over the side, Jesse urged the light mare back up into the air and out of the fissure.

Jesse looked back. Trapped in the bottom of the icy pit, the wolves snarled and snapped in vain.

Jesse and Daisy returned to the Vortex Interceptor at the same time. Daisy's light mare pranced, and Daisy's cheeks were rosy and her eyes shone.

"Why am I thinking you had more fun than I did?" Jesse said.

"You wanted to take the wolves," Daisy said.

"True," Jesse said. "Where's Emmy?"

"I saw them moving over that way," Daisy said, pointing with her feather duster toward the palace.

"Let's see if she needs our help," Jesse said.

Daisy and Jesse rode until they heard the sound of clashing metal. They soon came upon Emmy and Beowulf near the edge of the abyss, parrying and thrusting, Beowulf now with a sword of gold and Emmy with her unsheathed talons.

The Aurora bridge was gone. The Aurora now hovered overhead like spectators in a crowded airborne arena.

From what Jesse could see, it didn't look good for Emmy. Her talons had been sliced to the nub, while Beowulf looked as vigorous as ever, his golden sword flashing.

"Why doesn't she just zap him with her magic?" Daisy said.

"Maybe her magic isn't up to speed yet," Jesse said. "Maybe she has to rely on muscle until it gets there."

The Aurora sang out encouragement to Emmy:

Flame on, O dragon,
Like an emerald sun.
Melt the golden shaft
Of the Evil One!

"They're singing about Beowulf's golden sword!" Jesse cried out over the Aurora's song. "They're trying to tell her to flame it, and it will melt into a pile of goo. She must be too distracted to hear!"

Turning her sword into a megaphone, Daisy boomed, "Fight the sword with fire and melt it, Em!"

The next moment a ball of flame shot out of Emmy's mouth and struck the sword. Beowulf dropped the melting weapon and plunged his burned hand into the snow.

Emmy bore down upon him. Beowulf slipped and slid on the snow as he backed away from her.

"Back him right up into the abyss, Em!" Jesse shouted.

"Will do!" Emmy said.

Just then, the Aurora sang:

> The dragon prevails.
> The battle is done.
> The Army of Light
> Hath surely won.

Jesse and Daisy were both too tired to rhyme, so they slid off their mares' backs and watched as both their swords and their mounts disappeared back into the Aurora hovering overhead. By the Aurora's light, Jesse and Daisy could see that Beowulf was standing with his back to the edge of the precipice.

"Good-bye, B. O. Wolf," Emmy said. "It's been fun. *Not!*"

Emmy stuck out one hand and gave Beowulf a

shove. He teetered wildly, arms flailing, then fell backward into the abyss.

They waited for the scream. None came.

"I would have screamed my head off," said Jesse.

"Well," Daisy said, slapping the troll dust off her mittens, "that's one less dragon slayer to worry about."

Something was nagging Jesse. "Don't you think it was strange that he didn't even beg for his life?"

Emmy cradled her right paw with its sheared-off talons in the crook of her left arm. "Begging is beneath the dignity of your average Viking warrior," she said.

"But he didn't even seem scared," Jesse said.

"Warriors don't fear," said Emmy.

Jesse tried to shrug off his lingering anxiety.

Daisy said to Emmy, "Are you all right?"

"I'm fine," Emmy said. "Ichor will grow my talons back. See?" Emmy held up the damaged paw. Bright green liquid oozed from the stubs of her talons. Brand-new sharp talons sprang up.

"If you're feeling better," Daisy said, "I can show you where you hid the eggs."

Emmy's face lit up. "You found them?"

"When I climbed to the top of the Interceptor,

I'm pretty sure I discovered the spot," Daisy said.

"And you were going to tell me all this *when*?" Jesse said in a hurt tone.

"When I climbed down from the tower, but then the wolf started chasing us," Daisy said.

"Oh, right," said Jesse.

To Emmy, Daisy said, "This way."

Emmy and Jesse followed Daisy through the trampled snow until, not far from the edge of the abyss, they came to a hummock of snow the size of a kids' upturned wading pool. The hill was shaped like a big smiley face with two fangs.

"Good work, Daisy Flower!" Emmy said.

In two seconds, Emmy had dug away the smiley face and uncovered the brace of Thunder Eggs, which were held in a big net. They looked like a bag of softballs that had been rolled in oatmeal.

Emmy held up the bag and stared at it. "Now, if I could just figure out how to get these little suckers into that Interceptor gizmo and swivel the whosits to get the vortex thingie to whirligig in the right direction."

"What happened to all that technical talk you were spewing with the Claus?" said Jesse.

"The Claus's spell must have made me smarter about mechanical stuff than I really am," Emmy said. "I'm a magic girl, not a machine girl. All I know is that the Thunder Eggs were on their migratory path from the Time Before to the earth's core when I intercepted them. Unless I can get them back on their way to whichever realm they're meant to inhabit, they'll never hatch."

"Poor Ethereals!" Daisy said.

"How many are in there, anyway?" Jesse asked, peering into the net.

"Let's count them," said Daisy.

Jesse and Daisy were tallying up the Thunder Eggs when suddenly the ice beneath them began to tremble and shift. Then there came a loud series of creaks followed by a mighty boiling sound.

Emmy looked mystified. "That sounds like a volcano erupting."

The next moment, a Viking warship soared into view from the depths of the abyss. It was bristling with oars, and its red-and-gold-striped sail was unfurled. Carved into the bowsprit was a troll with fangs bared. Beowulf stood on the foredeck, arms folded across his chest. He threw back his head and laughed when he saw the looks on their faces.

"Fools! You've played right into my hands!"

Then he turned to face the ice palace. Arms raised high above his head, he intoned a chant.

The towers of the palace exploded, sending shards of ice flying high through the air. Jesse,

Daisy, and Emmy ducked. Then the ice beneath their feet began to heave and crack. With a cry, Daisy started to slide toward one of the gaping fissures.

Emmy reached out and caught her. They were all so distracted that no one noticed as Beowulf leapt from the deck of his ship to the ice, grabbed the net of Thunder Eggs, and leapt back aboard.

"The eggs!" Emmy cried.

CHAPTER TEN

GEATLAND

The three of them watched in utter dismay as the tip of the ship's mast disappeared back into the abyss.

"He was just waiting for us to uncover the eggs so he could steal them!" Emmy said. "And news flash—that isn't an abyss, it's a portal. Let's go."

Daisy walked to the edge of the portal and looked down. It was black and swirling like a tornado. It made a noise like a freight train pounding through a tunnel.

Daisy lifted her head to the lights and sang out loud and clear:

> In this scary portal
> we're about to land.
> We'd both feel better
> with swords in hand.

They held out their hands, and the light swords appeared.

"Thanks!" they both said. Jesse and Daisy took off their snowshoes and parked them on the edge of the portal. Then they climbed onto Emmy's back.

Without further ado, Emmy popped her wings and dropped like a big green stone into the portal.

The descent into the portal was more like riding white-water rapids than falling into a well. Emmy's body roiled and bucked against the current. Knuckles white and jaws clenched, Jesse and Daisy clung to her shoulder blades like a pair of rodeo riders hanging on to the horn of a bucking bronco's saddle.

Daisy was just getting the hang of staying on Emmy's back without wrenching her arms out of their sockets when something emerged from the whirling depths and came scuttling toward her on long hairy legs.

Daisy opened her mouth and screamed.

It was a tarantula the size of a giant tortoise. Moments later, a vampire swooped at her, flapping his long black cape and gnashing his fangs. A millipede soon followed, its thousands of toxic legs wriggling toward her.

When she had just about screamed herself hoarse, Jesse's scream pierced her eardrum. She looked over and saw that he was swatting at a green snake whipping around his head.

"Poisonous sea snake!" he cried, arms flailing.

Then a doctor in a white coat holding a long, dripping needle came at Jesse. "No shots!" Jesse pleaded.

Meanwhile, Emmy reared up as a wolf loomed before her. To Daisy, it was just a cartoon character and not scary at all. It was wearing overalls and red suspenders, licking its chops. It was the Big Bad Wolf from "The Three Little Pigs." As a small dragon, Emmy had been so afraid of that wolf that she had insisted on Jesse's taping a blank piece of paper over the picture in the book.

Daisy raised her sword to defend Emmy from the Big Bad Wolf. When she sliced through the wolf as if it were nothing, Daisy understood what was happening. She was afraid of millipedes and vampires and tarantulas. Jesse feared sea snakes and getting shots. And the otherwise fearless Emmy was afraid of the Big Bad Wolf.

Daisy called out to the other two: "Beowulf spelled the portal with things that scare us! But they're like scarecrows in a field. They're meant to frighten us away, but they're not real!"

"Thanks!" Emmy called back to her. She flew directly at the Big Bad Wolf, and the figment exploded around them like a burst balloon.

After that, they flew without flinching at the figments meant to send them scurrying back to the North Pole. Emmy also got the knack of working her tail like a rudder. It wasn't long before she was riding the portal's currents like a champion river rafter.

Ahead, Daisy saw a pinpoint of light. The pinpoint kept growing until they dropped out of the portal into a cold damp fog. The fog smelled of salt and fish and echoed with the screeching of gulls.

Gradually, the fog thinned. Beneath them, the vast gray surface of the ocean teemed with white waves. To the east, the sun rose up out of the ocean, looking like an unripe orange.

"It's dawn," Jesse said. "This is about as light as it's gonna get."

"This is Beowulf's home turf," Emmy said. "Geatland."

"Then this must be the North Sea," Jesse said. "At least that's where Geatland was in the legend."

Emmy flew toward an isolated mountain of streaked limestone jutting out of the sea. Clinging to the northernmost side of the peak was a castle with towers as jagged and grim as the rock out of which it had been hewn. Moored at the foot of the island was Beowulf's warship, its oars bristling like a millipede's legs, its red-and-gold-striped sail tightly furled.

"Coming in for a landing!" Emmy called out as she plummeted toward the parapet atop the castle keep.

As they drew nearer, Jesse saw that the battlements were manned with warriors clad in stiff leather skirts and vests and ox-horned helmets. When they spied Emmy, they swarmed back to the keep.

No sooner had Emmy set her feet down on the parapet, Jesse and Daisy tumbling off her back, than the first of the Viking warriors arrived, pounding up the narrow stone stairway.

"This ought to hold you," Emmy said to the cousins. She touched the tops of their heads. Instantly, they were clad in shiny green mail from head to foot.

"Dragon scales," Emmy said. "No sword can pierce them."

The Vikings rushed toward Jesse and Daisy, broadswords drawn. Their own light swords morphed into broadswords. Jesse and Daisy fought back to back as the warriors came at them, swinging and hacking with both hands. Meanwhile, Emmy hovered over the fray, plucking the most threatening warriors from the battlements and dropping them, kicking and screaming, into the North Sea. But as many Vikings as Emmy picked off, more came to take their places.

Suddenly, there came a sound like a foghorn blasting. Everyone froze, weapons in midair. Jesse looked down. Beowulf stood on the parapet below, one hand clutching a ram's horn, the other holding the net of Thunder Eggs.

"Surrender, Dragon!" he bellowed. "You are outnumbered."

Emmy roared in fury. "Never!"

Instantly, the broadswords resumed their hacking and slashing. Emmy flew down to the lower parapet and, with one sweep of her mighty tail, knocked Beowulf off his feet and into the side of the castle. She grabbed the net of eggs as they fell from his grip. Flying the net back up to the keep, she set it gently down. Then she returned to the dragon slayer, who was just regaining his feet, his face purple with rage.

Jesse and Daisy now had to fend for themselves. Jesse continued to meet the blows of the broadswords, but his arms were growing weak. Daisy's face was white and her hair beneath the dragon scale helmet was a wild tangle. Worse still, the Vikings had driven a wedge between them and they no longer had each other's backs.

A wall of Viking warriors drove them toward the battlement wall. One of the Vikings chopped at Jesse's wrist and his sword went clattering to the ground. Daisy, seeing Jesse lose his sword, flung hers down.

"We surrender," she said, raising her hands above her head.

Either the Vikings didn't understand the rules of war or the English language—or both—because they continued to back the Keepers up toward the wall, sword points at their throats.

Jesse opened his mouth and let out a feeble "Help!"

"Help!" Daisy joined him.

Together, they yelled with their remaining strength, "HELP! EMMY, HELP!"

From below, Emmy shouted, *"Yes!* I've *got* it!"

Jesse glanced over the parapet wall and caught sight of Emmy just as the dragon's eyes began to spin, blazing with a fierce and fearsome light. Beowulf staggered back, a look of genuine fear on his face. When the multicolored smoke from Emmy's nostrils disappeared, the entire Viking horde had vanished.

CHAPTER ELEVEN

REVERSE ACTION FIGURE SPELL

Jesse and Daisy straightened up and looked around. The parapet was littered with dozens of tiny plastic action figures.

Jesse picked one up and held it close to his face. Beneath its yellow mustache, the figure wore a deep scowl. Its elbows were jointed, and its little plastic broadsword could fit in either hand. Jesse worked the arm and made the sword swing in a small arc. "Cool!" he said.

Emmy flew up to join them. She touched the cousins' heads and their armor disappeared.

"I guess you finally got your full power back," Daisy said.

"Big-time," said Jesse.

"Aren't you two glad I had some practice being Santa's helper?" Emmy asked.

"What exactly did you do?" asked Jesse.

"Reverse Action Figure Spell," Emmy said with pride. "Worked like a charm, didn't it?"

"It sure did," said Jesse. "Where's Beowulf?"

Emmy shrugged. "Somewhere in this heap of plastic. These little dudes all look alike to me."

She walked over and picked up the bag of Thunder Eggs. "Let's get these back on track. To the North Pole on the double!"

"Oh, goody," said Jesse drily. "I can't wait."

"Do we have to go through that nasty portal?" Daisy asked.

"I think you'll find the portal quite changed," Emmy said.

With the net of Thunder Eggs clasped in her talons and her Keepers on her back, Emmy flew up toward the mouth of the giant gray funnel hovering in the sky over Geatland. Emmy was right. The trip back was like a pleasure cruise, the air filled with flitting butterflies, tweeting birds, and fragrant flowers.

When they emerged from the portal, Jesse and Daisy climbed down off Emmy's back. The very next moment, the great plates of ice began to move together with a scrape and a rumble, closing the portal to Geatland.

The Aurora greeted them in colorful splendor:

> We've sung of deeds both
>   bold and daring.
> Now we sing a song of joy.
> The Aurora is safe, as is the Ozone,
> Thanks to the dragon, the girl,
>   and the boy!

"Shucks," said Emmy. "It was nothing. Right, guys?"

Jesse and Daisy blushed, then sat down and put on their snowshoes. They were both feeling more than a touch of snow fatigue. Following Emmy, they trudged across the ice to Beowulf's Vortex machine.

"I sure hope she's figured out how to swivel the

whosits to get the thingie to whirligig in the right direction," Jesse said.

"I know exactly what you mean," said Daisy.

Emmy set the eggs down and slowly circled the Vortex Interceptor, all the time staring up at it. Then she threw back her head and directed a jet of flame at the bottommost girders. The metal turned bright yellow, then red, then finally white-hot. Like a flame traveling the length of a fuse, the white heat snaked up the Vortex machine. When it reached the top, there was a blinding flash. The next moment, the entire structure sagged, then collapsed through a hole in the ice, disappearing into the waters of the vast polar sea that lay beneath.

Emmy heaved a sigh of satisfaction. "Sometimes wrecking things is so much more fun than building them."

Jesse and Daisy were both mortified.

"What about the eggs?" Daisy asked.

"How will you get them back on track now?" Jesse asked.

"Who needs a Vortex Interceptor when you've got dragon magic?" Emmy said with a grin. She retrieved the net and rocketed with it back up into the air. Jesse and Daisy stood with their heads tilted back, eyes on the sky. For the longest time, nothing happened. Just when their necks were beginning to get stiff, the Aurora gathered directly above the spot where the Vortex Interceptor had been. This time, the light was green.

The green light formed itself into a long pipe, one end pointing into the sky and the other aimed at the hole in the ice. Through the pipe, the Thunder Eggs began to swirl down, moving in a clockwise spiral. One after another, the Ethereals wound down through the pipe and plummeted into the hole, until they were lost to sight.

When the last egg was gone, Emmy came rushing back to earth, the wind whistling through her wings. "The Ethereals are officially back on track!" she cried. "The Aurora are out of danger. And all's well with the world. Let's go home, Keepers."

"Plan," said Jesse and Daisy.

"Is it still Christmas?" Emmy asked hopefully as Jesse and Daisy climbed onto her back.

Jesse looked down at his wristwatch. "It's the day after. Four o'clock in the morning."

"It's Boxing Day!" Daisy announced.

Emmy brightened. "Does that mean I get to lace on the gloves and go a few rounds in the ring?"

"Silly girl," said Daisy. "Boxing Day is when people go to the store and return the gifts they don't like."

"How rude!" said Emmy.

"It's tradition," said Daisy.

"It's a rude tradition. But you haven't even *gotten* my gift yet," Emmy said.

"We told you," Jesse said. "You don't need to give us one."

"Having a dragon for Christmas is our gift," Daisy said.

"And having a Christmas adventure with you is something we'll never forget," said Jesse.

"Oh, but you don't understand!" Emmy said. "I finally found you guys the perfect gift. And I'm pretty sure you would never, ever *dream* of returning it."

After Emmy had flown them back to Goldmine City, she retired to the barn for a well-earned rest. But Jesse and Daisy couldn't rest yet. They woke up Aunt Maggie and Uncle Joe from their "long winter's nap," and got the delayed holiday festivities underway. By midmorning, Jesse and Daisy were sitting in a patch of buttery golden sunlight next to the Christmas tree in the living room. They were surrounded by a sea of crumpled wrapping paper and ribbons all sprinkled with Christmas cookie crumbs.

Uncle Joe said, "I think it's kind of a nifty break

with tradition waiting until the day after Christmas to open our gifts."

"I just don't know where yesterday went," Aunt Maggie said, mystified.

Daisy wagged a finger. "Too much Killer-Diller Loosey-Goosey Eggnog, Mom."

"I didn't have *that* much," Aunt Maggie said.

Uncle Joe frowned. "I might need to adjust the recipe. A little more goosey and a little less loosey."

"It's your turn to open, Mom," Daisy said. Hers was the last present under the tree.

Aunt Maggie unwrapped the mailing tube and pulled the paper out of the cylinder. She held the sparkling paper up to the light. "Red sparkles!" she said. "I love them. I'll use them to line my bureau drawers."

"Great idea, Mom," said Daisy.

Uncle Joe said, "And I'll use mine out in the Rock Shop, to line my specimen drawers."

"Perfect, Poppy," said Daisy, giving him a fond look.

In their stockings, the cousins had found the usual sensible or sentimental items: socks, tooth-brushes, candy canes, chocolate oranges, brain teasers, yo-yos. For bigger gifts, Jesse had gotten a coin collector's starter kit, a chemistry set, and stilts; Daisy had received a miniature loom, a fancy matching hairbrush and comb, and a pogo stick.

"I'm so sorry the snow is already melted, Jesse Tiger," said Aunt Maggie, giving him a sympathetic look.

Jesse smiled. "That's okay, Aunt Maggie. I got enough snow yesterday to last me a lifetime. Really."

"You have no idea," Daisy said under her breath.

"Hey, look!" said Uncle Joe, pointing beneath the lower tree branches. "There's one last present back there."

Uncle Joe pulled out a large gift, crudely wrapped in old newspaper and green duct tape. He read the tag: "To Jesse Tiger and Daisy Flower, from E of L." His eyes widened. "Very mysterious! Who's 'E of L'?"

Daisy was ready with an answer. "Elsa," she said. "She's a new girl in school."

"Really?" said Aunt Maggie. "Where is she from?"

Daisy shrugged. "Leandra!"

"Really? I've never heard of it. Where's that?" Uncle Joe asked.

Daisy frowned. "Up north. Norway, maybe? Yeah, that's it. Norway. You know, the land of Beowulf?"

"Well, why don't you kids open Elsa's gift?" said Aunt Maggie.

Jesse and Daisy tore away the newspaper. They found themselves staring at a plastic scale model of a Viking warship bristling with oars, its red-and-gold-striped sail unfurled, manned by a crew of tiny plastic Viking warriors.

"This guy here might be Beowulf himself," said Uncle Joe, picking up the action figure on the foredeck. Beneath the tiny helmet with the ox horns the figure had snow-white braids and a look of dread on his bearded face.

"Why not?" said Jesse.

"He doesn't look so tough to me," Daisy said.

"Say!" said Uncle Joe, returning Beowulf to the foredeck. "The detail on this ship is impressive! It looks really authentic."

"These European toy makers," Aunt Maggie said with an admiring shake of her head. "Santa's workshop can't match them for quality."

"Hey, Jess," said Daisy. "Check out the bowsprit."

Instead of the goblin with the fangs, there was now a dragon with green scales and emerald-green eyes.

Uncle Joe regarded it doubtfully. "I'm not sure

how many enemies that cream puff is going to scare away," he said.

"Oh, I think that cream puff can hold her own," said Jesse. "Don't you, Daise?"

Daisy grinned widely. "Totally!"

Dear Mom and Dad, Christmas in America
was amazing. The good news is that it
snowed! And more than just a dusting!
The bad news is that it melted overnight.
I hope you guys liked your gifts. Did you know
that paper was one of the most ingenious
inventions in the history of the world? Daisy
and I got lots of neat presents, but the
neatest one (next to my new Blueberry)
was a model of a Viking warship. One of the
crewmen even looks like Beowulf. Except that
he doesn't look very brave. In fact, he looks
scared stiff. Maybe it's the dragon carved
into the bowsprit. Daisy and I are going to
keep it in the barn, along with our other
treasures. We're headed up there right now
to test Daisy's new pogo stick.
Merry Christmas,
Your son in America,
Jesse Tiger

KATE KLIMO has always believed that Santa Claus is the ultimate and, for many of us, the very first fantasy hero in our lives. When she was a child, she always stayed up late the night before Christmas to see if she could hear the ringing of sleigh bells or the rumble of reindeer's hooves on the roof. To this day, she thinks there is something about Christmas that's just a little bit more magical than any other day of the year.

One Christmas Day, when she was horseback riding in the park, she came upon a jolly old man in a long white beard and a fur-trimmed red suit galloping along on a white stallion strewn with sleigh bells. She hopes you will find some of that holiday magic in this latest Dragon Keepers adventure.

Kate lives in New Paltz, New York, with her husband and horses. For more information, visit FoundaDragon.org and TheDragonKeepers.com.